OREOS AND A PACK OF MARLBORO LIGHTS

Oreos and a Pack of Marlboro Lights

A collection of stories

by

JEFFREY KASS

Adelaide Books
New York/Lisbon
2019

OREOS AND A PACK OF MARLBORO LIGHTS
A collection of stories
By Jeffrey Kass

Copyright © by Jeffrey Kass
Cover design © 2019 Adelaide Books

Published by Adelaide Books, New York / Lisbon
adelaidebooks.org

Editor-in-Chief
Stevan V. Nikolic

For any information, please address Adelaide Books
at info@adelaidebooks.org
or write to:
Adelaide Books
244 Fifth Ave. Suite D27
New York, NY, 10001

ISBN-10: 1-950437-64-7
ISBN-13: 978-1-950437-64-1

Printed in the United States of America

Contents

Introduction

Oreos and a Pack of Marlboro Lights is a collection of true stories, essays, and even a poem, which have only been lightly fictionalized to protect some of my innocent—or should I say guilty muses. The book is intended to entertain, make you laugh, and even make you say a few "oh shits!" To instigate, to inspire, to think, to challenge, and to deep dive into the psyche. To a few times make you reflect on your own life. The stories span many years and cover a wide variety of subjects including relationships, race, religion, and coming of age matters.

This book came about through an essay contest I entered through the publisher Adelaide Books. I had just finished a fifteen-chapter traumedy memoir, *Sheldon & Irene,* and decided to submit chapter one in the competition. I was about to embark on the arduous task of finding an agent for my book but decided I needed some street cred before anyone would take me seriously. I had won and placed as a finalist in several international writing competitions over the past year and a half, but felt that submitting chapter one of my book would provide the encouragement I needed to keep improving the book. Lo and behold, that chapter, called "Staycation," won the 2018 competition. One of the prizes was a book publishing contract for a collection of essays and stories, yet to be written. That's when

I embarked on this project and over the ensuing six months, wrote the chapters to *Oreos and a Pack of Marlboro Lights.*

I want to give a special thanks first and foremost to my parents. Their intentional and yes, sometimes unintentional, education provided me with a foundation of love, constitution, confidence and justice that has guided me throughout my life. I also thank my brother who has been my rock and best friend since we stopped hitting each other when I was twelve and his eight-year-old self learned to punch back. I owe additional thank-yous to several dear friends who always keep me on the path of laughter, social consciousness, and love. Aaron, Joseph, Ryan, Jeff, Mario, Chris, Allen, John, Dean Sr. and Laura, just to name a few. Their support through life's constant challenges has kept me grounded. As weird as it may seem, I am thankful for an ex-girlfriend, Leigha, who not always on purpose helped me dig deeper into my psyche than ever before. I also want to thank Nicole Holcomb, who edited my stories and provided me with oftentimes profound comments. She has made me a better writer. While I typically keep them out of my stories, and hopefully the trauma of my stories, I also thank my beautiful, kind, smart, curious and delightful kids. The miracle, wonder and love they add to my life is like no other and I would not be the man I am today without them. They make me want to be a better person every day. They have taught me the true meaning of unconditional love.

My hope is that the stories in this book engage you as you smile, growl, laugh and love through their pages. Most of all, I hope the stories inspire you to be a light in a world oftentimes fraught with the darkness of personal and political challenges. One thing I've learned through this first half of life is we can't control others, but we can control our actions and reactions to life's events.

Finally, I owe tremendous gratitude to Adelaide Books, Adelaide Literary Magazine, and their editor Stevan Nikolic, who have given me this tremendous opportunity to showcase my writing and help propel what I hope is a long and successful writing career.

1

Twenty-Four Inches

Jessica really didn't give me much guidance on what we'd be doing at the prison. All she knew was that I was prone to supporting good causes, so she asked if I'd support her by volunteering at some state prison in the middle of nowhere Colorado. "It's an entrepreneur training program for prisoners to help prepare them for when they reenter society," she explained. I gathered she also asked me to help out because of my experience helping entrepreneurs as part of my law practice. Vince, a successful business man with similar social justice ideals as me, had planned to volunteer as well, so we carpooled for the two-hour drive.

The only other time I had been to a prison was when my friend James brought drugs to a party and a girl overdosed and died after taking them. She had taken drugs all night so the drugs James gave her put her over the top. He wasn't trying to harm anyone, but you can't really call it an accident when people regularly die of overdoses of hardcore drugs. He had to serve five years in a federal minimum security prison in Arkansas. My visit to James in prison wasn't a pleasant experience even as a guest. It didn't help that James told me about the gangs and violence there. I remember thinking at the time that if this was a minimum security facility, I'd hate to see a maximum one.

"Any clue what we're going to be doing at the prison, Vince?" I asked in a crap-why-did-I-sign-up-for-this tone.

"No idea. I think it's a program they're doing for prisoners and we're just there to support it."

"Are you kidding me? I'm driving two hours to sit in an audience and then have someone ask me for a donation if I like what I see? I would've given them a check without taking a day off work," I told Vince, increasingly annoyed. Work was super busy and I wasn't thrilled about taking an entire day off for something I knew almost nothing about. It wasn't like me to get so bent out of shape, but I kind of felt like I was being taken advantage of because of my liberal bleeding heart. It wouldn't have been the first time I was suckered into donating or helping out.

After two hours of Vince reluctantly tolerating my uncharacteristic complaining, we arrived at the silver barbed-wire, fenced-in, giant concrete prison. What I hadn't been told is that the prison was what they call a "super max" prison. An über-maximum security to the 'nth degree prison only for the most violent criminals. Many of the prisoners sit in solitary confinement twenty-three hours a day. You heard me. Like those caged-in animals at the small reptile exhibit at the St. Louis Zoo I used to visit with my kids. When I learned of the type of prison we were visiting, it didn't exactly warm me to this so-called "volunteering." Weren't these the worst of the worst, beyond help?

After a brief introduction by the personnel running the day's program, a set of dos and don'ts, and some vague background on what would be taking place, we headed into the fortress known as prison.

"What's that music playing?" I asked one of the other volunteers as I heard *I gotta feeling that tonight's gonna be a good night...* by The Black Eyed Peas blasting in the distance. We just looked at each other confused. She didn't know either. What kind of high security prison was this? We got off the elevator and the music was even louder. Like a South Beach nightclub where they make people stand in line for an extra hour just to make them think something exclusive and exciting was happening inside. The volunteers in front of me picked up speed as we were now jogging into a room with twenty men in beige prisoner jumpsuits greeting us by forming a human tunnel with high fives like we were just introduced as the starting lineup of the Golden State Warriors. What the... I had no idea what was about to go down. This didn't seem like the start of a boring infomercial after all.

Far from sitting through a boring program, we were called upon to be thoroughly engaged with the prisoners throughout the day focused on business, self-worth, and value coaching. What I didn't know at the beginning was that my life was about to be changed forever.

The day consisted of many activities. Ice breakers eased us into getting to know each other. We checked off boxes on a piece of paper when a volunteer and prisoner had the same answer to a personal question. Where did you grow up? What's your favorite sports team? How many siblings do you have? What letter does your first name begin with? Those types of meaningless things, but enough to get us all talking. The prisoners each had smiles on their faces, eager to connect. Some had not been visited by anyone in years, so the company of random strangers felt good to them. After the icebreakers, each volunteer paired up with a prisoner for ten to fifteen minutes at a time to go over business and marketing plans for ideas the prisoners developed for when they got out of prison. Mobile car detailing services. Commercial cleaning. Transportation services. Each prisoner had been working extensively on real plans. It was actually quite impressive.

Then the day's program took a sharp turn. We were no longer discussing improvements to personal statements or business plans. Instead, the prisoners were all asked to go to one wall, backs against it. The volunteers, facing the prisoners, all went to the opposite wall. The room was nondescript. White walls. Gray carpet. No art work. No furniture. Just a blank room. Each volunteer and prisoner were asked to look at their assigned partner across the room during this exercise. A purple line of tape was placed the length of the room about ten feet in front of the volunteers. Red tape was placed in parallel to the purple tape, also about ten feet in front of the prisoners. The red and purple lines of tape were a mere two feet from each other.

"Okay," the facilitator Jen from Nashville started with her charming southern accent. "I'm going to ask some questions. If you answer yes to the question, I want you to step to the line in front of you. Volunteers step to the purple line. EITs step to the red tape." EITs was short for entrepreneurs in training. "Remember to look at your partner," they told us and the EITs. Calling the prisoners EITs instead of inmates obviously was a form of encouragement and respect.

"If you've lost a parent before the age of eighteen, please step to the line."

A shocking five of the twenty volunteers and thirteen of the prisoners stepped to their respective lines facing each other.

"Next one. If there's something you've been unable to forgive yourself for, step to the line."

Sixteen volunteers and all twenty prisoners stepped to their lines, again facing each other.

The exercise went on for another forty minutes, each time the questions increasing with seriousness and impact. Each time with several volunteers and prisoners simultaneously stepping to the dreaded colored lines. Not even sure why they had to use such nice colors for this exercise. Purple tape? Really?

"Have you ever lost a child?"

One thirty something year old prisoner, Darius, stepped to the red line. Darius was in prison for stabbing someone during an argument. He had a pleasant demeanor and warm smile. He was African American with tattoos down both arms. Glasses. Caring eyes. An infectious smile. One volunteer, no older than thirty-five, Becca, stepped to the purple line. She was a rising star hedge fund manager. Short, maybe five-foot one. Straight brown hair and compassionate looking green eyes. A soft demeanor. Becca and Darius were about five feet down from each other, but they moved to face each other since they were the only two who answered yes to this harrowing question. We were only allowed to fist pump or shake hands with the prisoners, but the two stood there, tears in their eyes, holding a tightly squeezed, all-hands "handshake" together for a solid three minutes. There wasn't a dry eye in the house. Seemed like the no-hugging rule should have been relaxed for this moment.

While it wasn't lost on me that Darius and the other prisoners had done some awful things, I was taken aback by how most of them got there. Darius was eleven years old when he first entered the American so-called justice system. While witnessing his dad beating his mom with a leather belt, Darius took a knife and put it in the middle of his dad's back. "Leave Mom alone!" he shouted as he pushed the knife in as hard as he could and twisted it. I never took a knife out, but I recall feeling the same way Darius felt when my own dad cheated on my mom with a woman eight houses down from us. Instead of being rescued from an abusive environment, Darius was arrested, labeled a criminal, and put into the juvenile justice system. The rest of his criminal life is history.

The next question asked by Jen came hard and fast like a lightning bolt. I wasn't ready for it.

"Have you ever thought about committing suicide?"

I hesitated as I looked around the room at the other professionals. Nine of the volunteers stepped forward. A CEO, a lawyer, a banker, and a few business owners. Nineteen of the prisoners moved forward. But I froze. Never in my forty-nine years had I ever discussed what I felt as a eleven-year old when I discovered Dad's escapades. Now I was being asked to disclose that information publicly? I looked around the room again, embarrassed but certainly not alone. I wanted to lie and just stay still, but instead I slowly walked to the line and looked at the tears in the eyes of Gomez, the prisoner directly across from me, as he empathetically stared back into the tears now pouring down my own face. Gomez had shot a man during a robbery. He was only forty-two, but had a face that was two decades older. Tired and worn. He was only five-foot six, and about twenty pounds overweight. His eyes were filled to the brim of sorrow, apology, and forgiveness. We gently shook hands and just stayed and stared into each other. Aside from the faint whimpers of the reluctant crying of a few grown men, you could hear a pin drop in the room. So much pain and regret filled our collective hearts.

I don't really recall the rest of the day, but it dawned on me as Vince and I headed home to Denver that I was a mere twenty-four inches away from making a bad decision and ending up in front of the red line instead of the purple one.

2

Oreos and a Pack of Marlboro Lights

"Freeze boy!" the officer shouted as he drew his 9mm handgun and pointed it right at the kid's head.

The white, plain-clothed police officer dressed in blue jeans and a black polo raced his unmarked navy blue Dodge Charger to a screeching halt right behind the Chevy Camaro rental car I had just parallel parked along the west side of South Boyle Avenue, off Manchester Road. I was in St. Louis for work and was headed to eat at one of my favorite local dinner spots, Sanctuaria. Their version of "fish n' chips" is a corn-cake breaded mahi-mahi with jicama fries. But my growling stomach was no longer on my mind.

A second plain-clothed cop dressed in beige khaki pants, a blue polo shirt, and Kevin Durant Nike tennis shoes emerged from the Charger.

"Turn around, boy!" he said in a stern voice. He patted down and searched the nineteen or twenty-year-old black kid. His groin. His legs. Arms. Everywhere.

I stayed in my car, partially out of fear, partially to make sure nothing awful went down. By this time, I had cracked the window on the passenger's side of my rental car, the side closest to the sidewalk where the two cops and young man were standing. In the subtlest way I could, I aimed my iPhone video camera at the passenger side mirror of my car. The side mirror was pointed directly at the cops and kid. I wasn't looking to make the 6:00 news, but I thought it would be a good idea to document what was taking place, even though I wasn't quite sure what that was yet.

"I'm going to handcuff you while we ask you a few questions, okay?" The officer didn't wait for a response. Instead, he took out a pair of handcuffs stuffed in his utility belt and closed them on the boy's hands. They weren't the metal, silver looking kind of handcuffs you see in older movies. They were clear, plastic, and tied tight like those nylon cables I use on my flagpole in my front yard to make sure my flag doesn't blow away.

"Ouch, that hurts!" the boy complained.

"That's what happens when you cross us. Did you have a gun?" the officer asked in an increasingly harsh voice.

"No," the kid responded, almost in a fuck-you tone.

"We saw you throw a gun into the bushes when you spotted us watching you."

"Man, I didn't even know y'all were watchin' me and don't even own a gun." The boy had started raising his voice at this point.

The second officer left to search the shrubs, grass, and surrounding areas for at least an entire block south down Boyle. Scoured the place.

"I can't find anything, Jo Jo," he shouted to his partner in a disappointed tone. On his return, obviously coming up empty, he returned to take over the questioning. "You have two choices.

We can sit here all day with you in handcuffs until you come clean about what the hell you're up to, or you can cooperate and make this easy. Sounds like an easy decision if ya ask me."

"Why you trippin'? Just on my way to the convenience store to buy some snacks and joes." The kid had stopped his sarcasm and his tone turned to frightened.

The kid was about 5'10", thin, had a medium dark brown complexion with a few tiny black moles on the side of his face, and a short, disheveled afro. Probably hadn't shaved in two to three days. Striking green eyes. He wore baggy jeans—you know the kind that droop almost down to the back of the knees. The kind I always thought looked ridiculous on people. He had on a white t-shirt, dark bomber jacket, and slightly worn white Adidas tennis shoes with three black stripes on each side. The shoes were the newest looking article of clothing on his body.

It was a bit of a cool day for St. Louis for late May. Fifty-five degrees and almost no humidity. I may have never moved from St. Louis had most days been that pleasant. Usually by May it was so hot and humid a person would sweat profusely just walking a block. "Looks like I brought you our beautiful Colorado weather," I told my friend Aaron hours earlier. Amazing how a couple years in Colorado changed my level of tolerance from the brutal humidity of the Midwest. If you can call St. Louis and its southern mentality the Midwest.

"Let me see your driver's license, boy!"

I didn't understand why only now they were interested in who this kid was.

"Man, I told you, I was just walking to the convenience store to buy some cookies and smokes."

The kid reached into his pocket. "Here," and handed the cop his ID.

The first officer took the license back to his car. Within a few minutes, he came back with a look of increased disappointment on his face. "You lucky bastard. No record." He paused for a few seconds. "Yet. But you're gonna get a record if you don't come clean about what you're up to."

The boy didn't answer. Just gave the officers a "what's the use in repeating myself" kind of look. Another several minutes went by with the two cops chatting about their next move.

"Unlock him, Lance," his partner Jo Jo said in a resigned voice. Officer Lance fumbled through his coat jacket and pouch. "I can't find the damn keys. Shit!"

The other officer went back to the car, and after a few more minutes, finally returned with a set of keys. "I found 'em!" They mumbled something else to the boy as he left headed in the same direction before his detention. "We'll be watching you," was the cop's departing words to the kid.

The officers left the scene, but I stayed in the car, heart racing. Though I was never in any danger myself, I knew the cops wouldn't have been too happy if they knew I had recorded the whole thing. It took a few more minutes, but my breathing and heartbeat finally slowed as my nerves quickly turned to anger. I called my friend Ryan in Denver. Then Joe in Atlanta. Reggie in New York. I always had more black friends than the typical white guy, and felt like I had to share what had just transpired. "You're not going to believe what I just witnessed," I started out each call. Of course, none of my friends responded with surprise, though I had felt the urgency to share burning in my chest.

Just as I was wrapping up my last call and preparing to finally go to dinner, I looked up to see the kid walking past my car, back toward the direction from which he originally came. Only this time he had a cigarette in his hand and he was carrying a plastic bag that read "N&M Mart" on the side.

I decided to approach him.

"Hey, kid, may I ask you what happened twenty minutes ago? Are you okay?"

"Man, same ole shit, different day. Fourth time this damn month they stopped me," he said in a forfeited tone.

"Why were they questioning you?" I curiously asked, genuinely wanting to get to the bottom of things. I only was able to make out part of the interaction while it was happening.

"They said they saw me throw a gun into the bushes. Total bullshit. I told 'em I don't even own a damn gun. My brother used to own one, but he's in jail now and I didn't want to end up like that. Ty don't even get to see his baby. The whole thing is fucked up. They arrested him walking after some neighbors called the police, saying they saw some black kid walking around. That shit coulda been me."

As I was driving back after dinner, still in deep thought from what had transpired earlier, a trooper pulled me over for speeding down Skinker Boulevard. I've been known to have a heavy foot. The red Camaro I rented probably hadn't helped my cause.

"Do you know how fast you were going," the officer asked me after I rolled down my window.

"I was just flowing with traffic," I annoyingly said to the officer. I already was running late to meet my friend Aaron and his wife for a drink and the thought of spending twenty minutes parked on the side of the road was starting to bother me.

"Registration, license and insurance, please."

"It's a rental car, but here's my license and insurance card." I unlatched my seat belt and reached into my front pocket to grab the license and insurance card from my wallet as the officer stood outside the window patiently waiting. I handed them to the cop. "Here you go. I'm just visiting St. Louis and really didn't know I was speeding, officer."

"Stay in your car. I'll be back in a few minutes," he responded.

As promised, he returned with my license and insurance. "Do me a favor, slow down. I'm just going to give you a warning this time. Enjoy your stay in St. Louis."

"Thank you, officer. I'll be more careful." And then I drove off.

3

Fat or Flat Tire

"You're not going to believe this, Jeffrey! My car just broke down. I'm stuck at the Johnstown exit. Going to call Tom to come help. He's a mechanic friend. I've known him for years. We never dated or anything so you have nothing to worry about. He used to fix our cars when I was married. Heck, I never even cheated on my husband. Anyway, I'm so sorry I can't make it today after all. Please tell Gabrielle I am sorry too. I was so looking forward to seeing you guys."

It seemed a bit bizarre to me that Jennifer's 2016 Jeep Cherokee had broken down. Even though she bought it used, the car was just over a year old and had a measly 24,000 miles on it. This was the third time Jen had canceled a date with me in the last two weeks. This time felt worse because she was supposed to go to the zoo with my daughter and me. I rarely introduce women I date to my kids and started regretting having done so with Jen. Something seemed off.

"Sorry, Gabby," I told my daughter. "Jen can't make it today. Her car broke down." Gabby was only twelve, but she

23

had trouble buying the story too. "But her car isn't old, Tatty. Did it really break down?" Tatty is a Jewish word for dad, and that's what my kids have called me since they could speak. It always sounded more affectionate to me than "dad" anyway, although ironically, it weirds out some of my Jewish friends. My Christian and Muslim friends find it endearing, as do I. "So awesome you are in tune with your own culture" is a common refrain from them.

Jen lived about an hour away from me, so our first date four months earlier was at a sushi restaurant somewhere between my house in Denver and hers in Greeley, Colorado. I met her on the dating app Bumble. I usually don't get all that intrigued from online dating profiles, but Jen's stood out. Not only was she physically stunning, she wrote in her profile about valuing kindness, integrity, volunteering, and giving back. Certainly a step up from the typical "fun loving" and "I love my family and friends" clichés. It had been four years since I was genuinely interested in anyone, so I was probably more excited than I should've been before even meeting Jen.

When she arrived for our first date on Thursday, October 12, 2017, she was even more beautiful than her pictures. Long, gorgeous brown hair. Alluring, almost glowing, green eyes. A couple of cute freckles around her nose. Long eyelashes, which I later learned were fake. She was a yoga instructor, so her body was lean and stunning too. We had spent hours talking on the phone for two weeks before meeting, and felt as though we already had a strong connection, so I did something I only do when I am super excited at the beginning of a first date. I leaned over and gave her a hello kiss. She reciprocated.

"Wanna get some sake, Jeffrey?" was the first thing she said when we sat down. "Ummm… sure," I hesitated. I wasn't thrilled about drinking and then having to drive forty minutes back to Denver on a work night, but I figured a few sips of sake would be okay. I had a small glass from the carafe we ordered. Jen quickly disposed of the rest. "We'll have another carafe," she told the server a mere fifteen minutes after we ordered the first one. I didn't have any more sake, but Jen guzzled down the entire second carafe by herself. I was never into substances, so the quantity she consumed caught my attention. I didn't think sake was all that high in alcohol content, so I ultimately ignored the first date drinking since the evening was otherwise a great success.

We talked and talked and talked. She held my hand. Even sat next to me at dinner. She said all the right things. I hadn't felt so comfortable with someone in so long. She shared deep personal stories including her loss of a child at birth. The death of her dad three years ago. She didn't hold back. Just open heart sharing. I shared as well, telling her about the impact my dad's cheating had on me.

"You have nothing to worry about here, Jeffrey. I've never cheated on anyone in my life. You can even talk to my ex-husband. He'll tell you how loyal I am." That sounded like a big enough endorsement to me.

We sat in my car and kissed for fifteen minutes before we both went our opposite directions. "Will you text me when you get home, so I know you're safe?" I asked Jen. I drove home smiling the entire way. I couldn't believe it. I had just met a gorgeous, kind, fun, loyal woman. I'd waited so long for this! I was in heaven. Jen texted me a half hour later: "I'm home! Thanks again for a perfect evening. Can't wait to see you again." My heart was melting.

Jen and I met again a few days later, this time just outside of Greeley in Fort Collins. I took her to one of the nicer restaurants there, The Kitchen, and we again just talked nonstop and held hands, laughed and smiled. I wanted to pinch myself I was so excited, until she ordered her fifth beer. They were the tall, curved ale glasses too. I politely inquired, "Are you okay to drink that much?" "Oh, five beers is nothing for me. I need at least ten to get drunk" she calmly bragged without blinking an eye. Ten beers? I'd be on the floor or getting my stomach pumped at the ER if I drank that much, I thought to myself. I was once engaged to someone who drank a ton… it didn't turn out so well for me. Still, Jen remained kind and affectionate. So I decided to ignore the drinking again. Well, sort of.

Jen drove to my house for the next few dates, each time stopping at the liquor store on the way there, showing up with a few six packs or a bottle of vodka. Each time we had fun, but each time Jen got drunk, sometimes to the point of not being able to complete a coherent sentence. Or in some instances turning downright mean, without even remembering the next day what awful things she said.

One time after watching a movie in my basement and having sex on my couch, Jen abruptly started yelling at me. "Should we even be dating," she barked. Still in denial over her drinking, I was stunned. "What?" was all I could muster. Jen had downed four vodka club sodas that night.

"Why did you ask me if we should even be dating after such a nice evening?" I asked her as she woke up in my bed the next morning.

"Did I say that? Sorry. Must've been the vodka talking. I shouldn't drink that stuff."

The worst was when we went out in public. "Are you looking at that woman?" she would ask me several times in an accusatory tone while she'd been drinking. Each time I reminded and reassured her that she was the prettiest woman in the room and I had no desire to look at anyone else, but my level of irritation increased each time.

"What the hell is going on with you, always accusing me of doing something wrong. Always criticizing me!" When Jen drank, she criticized my every move and it didn't feel good. For my own messed up reasons, I don't do well with nonstop criticism.

I knew very little about alcoholism, so I began taking it all very personally, increasing in irritation each time. I was smart enough to know Jen had a problem, but I couldn't separate that from how she was treating me. My heart was already partially invested, long before my brain had a chance to catch up. A recipe for disaster. A part of me wanted to just end things, which I would try to do several times over the course of our six-month relationship, but a part of me was intoxicated as well—by Jen.

"I'm a little worried about your drinking, Jen," I would try approaching the subject.

"I don't really feel like being judged, Jeffrey. I want to be with someone who just accepts and loves me for who I am," she defiantly told me over and over.

I couldn't let that go. "Who you are? I do accept you for the kind, affectionate, beautiful woman you are. But is drinking who you are?" I asked her. "Is that how you define yourself?"

"Of course not." She backed off.

These types of exchanges went on for the entire first month of our relationship, all the while Jen's drinking increased each day.

"My kids are asleep. I can talk to you now," she texted me one evening after we'd been dating just a month.

Jen had two beautiful girls. Madison was six and had bright shiny blonde hair, presumably from her dad's side. A bit of a firecracker with a strong personality, but still fun. Paige was nine, smart, and engaging. She was an old soul. Both were adorable and had an intelligence beyond their years.

"Jen, you can't even complete a thought. You're slurring your words!"

"Fuck you! I don't need you judging me. I'm tired of you trying to control me," she said in a mumbled but angry voice, always forgetting that when sober, she acknowledged her alcoholism. After every alcohol-induced big fight, Jen would text me the next day, "Good morning baby!!" as if nothing had taken place.

It took me a few months to accept it, but Jen had been drunk for most nights of the three months we had now been together. Didn't matter if she was with her kids or alone. Didn't matter if it was a Tuesday or Saturday night. As our arguments over her drinking intensified, and after already three times trying to end things with Jen, she began disappearing and canceling dates. And when I say disappearing, I mean literally no contact from six in the evening until the next morning.

"I tried texting and calling last night. Where did you go?"

"I went drinking with Callie." "I went over to Jess's house to drink." "I went for dinner and drinks with Amy." Etc. Etc. Etc. The explanations were the same.

Jen had still texted me cute little hellos or thinking-about-yous up until this point, but that had all come to an end. I began wondering if Jen was seeing someone else. She insisted it was just the drinking. I instinctively knew the drinking had led to other bad decisions as well, but I couldn't be honest with myself. It hurt too much, which is kind of silly since I barely knew her, but I had my own issues as well.

The drinking wasn't the only thing that made me worry about whether Jen was cheating or sleeping with random men met at bars. Jen loved the attention of men. Always posting selfies online to solicit comments and sexual responses from them. Always getting emails, Facebook and Instagram messages, and texts from men pursuing her. Random guys. Ex-boyfriends. One 275-pound bald guy, Bill, figured out a way to keep Jen's attention by ordering products from her company. According to Jen, she desperately needed money since she never got alimony or much child support from her well-to-do ex-husband in her divorce, so she explained that she couldn't turn down the business even if some of it was from men who wanted more than just logo-imprinted coffee mugs. It didn't matter to Jen that one client had made it clear that he wanted to be with her and he wasn't going to give up just because she had a boyfriend. It was always, "I need the money."

"Who are you texting?" I demanded to know when she went upstairs in my house to send some messages ten minutes after we had sex on my living room couch.

Jen had become more and more secretive, which made me more and more insecure. "Will you stop, Jeffrey. I'm not with any other men. I would never do that to you. That's disgusting. That was just Bill texting me about his order of business cards for his law firm. He's gross anyway. 275 pounds!"

"At ten o'clock at night in my house?"

Jen's denials increased with intensity. Not coincidentally, her date cancellations and disappearances increased as well.

"You're not going to believe this, Jeffrey, but my kids' grandmother just had a stroke. I am so sorry to cancel, but I have to pick up the kids from my ex's house."

"I got a flat tire! Crap. Let's reschedule for this weekend."

"My friend Katie just broke up with her boyfriend. I need to stay with her and console her. So sorry."

I finally caught Jen lying about where she was one evening, and she finally confessed—sort of—to having lied about all the other excuses for canceling. There was no stroke. No broken down car. No breakup. No flat tire. Jen explained that she was out getting drunk each of those times. Since I knew she drank heavily, I foolishly bought her story and stayed with her. The alcohol story seemed plausible. But it was far worse than that.

After attempting to break up with Jen again over her lies, drinking and disappearing, each time Jen begging me to stay, I finally couldn't take it anymore and told her this was it. Jen had pleaded with me to stay with her so many times, but this was different. I was ready to walk. Some of the earlier breakup attempts were scary. She once said she wanted to kill herself if she couldn't have me, while drunk of course. She told me on our five-month anniversary that she couldn't imagine a life without me. That she wanted a baby with me. That she was going to get sober, go into an outpatient treatment program and do what it took to be present. She promised to spend the following day with me to begin that process. "I'm ready to get better, be present, stop disappearing, and give you the love you deserve," she assured me in the same convincing tone she used to lie about the stroke. "I will drive down tomorrow and start being with you from now on." And of course I bought her story again… until it happened.

Ring. Ring.

"Hey babe!"

"Oh I hate to do this, Jeffrey, but my daughter Madison is in the hospital ER with severe stomach pains."

"Jen, you know this is not going to go well if you're lying." It might have seemed insensitive for that to be the first thing out of my mouth, but Jen had told so many lies that I had trouble believing anything she said. I felt bad for not first hoping her daughter was okay, but I knew in the depths of my heart that this was just another lie.

"Lying? I know I've done you wrong in the past, and I've lied about my drinking, but this is the truth and I would never lie about one of my own kids being in the hospital. That would be sick."

Jen always knew how to make me feel like I was going crazy when I accused her of lying. Like I'm the one who had the problem. As if I was being insecure without justification. Every ounce of me knew she was lying again, but I had to know for sure. So when Jen disappeared and didn't respond to the calls or texts immediately following the ER excuse, I did the unthinkable. I called Jen's ex-husband and asked him point blank. "Is your daughter Madison okay?" "Of course," he said. "She and Paige are with my mom and fiancée." I felt like an idiot calling her ex-husband, but I didn't know what else to do. I had to know for sure.

I immediately emailed Jen to tell her not to contact me anymore. That I knew she wasn't getting sober and that she for sure was having a full-on affair, cheating and lying, and I never wanted to see her again. Indeed, her ex told me she already had been introducing another guy as her boyfriend at school events for her kids for over two months. All while having her kids spend time with me, too. I meant it this time. I was done with her. Later that night, Jen emailed back to finally come clean, as if I needed her to. She had been seeing one of her "clients," Bill, at the same time as me for three months, telling me "You wouldn't understand. I needed the money." Bill, the heavyset, wealthy bald lawyer, was giving Jen loads of cash to be with him. He actually put $1,500 cash in her purse one day. Paid some of her bills. Got the kids presents Jen couldn't afford. Pure prostitution.

I literally vomited.

I couldn't figure out what sick kind of person would beg and beg and beg me to stay with her for the last three months, only to cheat in exchange for money. I had given Jen an out over and over when I tried to leave, each time with her telling me she can't imagine a future without me.

At the end of the day, I was angrier with myself than I was at Jen. For having ignored the alcoholism. Half-believing the repeated and obvious lies. Accepting that her cravings for male attention was okay.

Fortunately, this was one of the easier breakups to get through. I wasn't falling in love. I was in lust. At no time have I ever looked back and said, "Well, that one got away from me." Even after she reached out to me a month after the breakup with a random "Hey Jeffrey!" text—as if I would somehow want to have such a person in my life again. I didn't respond, but I did hear that the lawyer who gave her $1,500 got her pregnant. I'm grateful I didn't learn about her escapades years into a marriage, like her ex-husband learned the hard way when she did the same thing to him.

The only good thing now is I can finally enjoy a cocktail again.

4

Thank you, Jackie!

"Get your paws off me!"

I wanted to cry, but Jason, who was only three feet from me, was a bit of a bully. If he saw me shed a tear after Jackie pushed me off her during my first ever kiss in a game of spin-the-bottle, I would've never made it through the rest of seventh grade. What did I know about kissing anyway? I was twelve, and the only kissing I knew was from *General Hospital*, where the man usually mauls his lovers with passionate, five-minute long, heavy breathing, full mouth-body moving kissing sessions. Mom and Dad never made out in front of Aaron or me so that was my only frame of reference. I thought I'd be a pro after two years of watching soap operas, but it didn't quite work out that way.

"You are such a violent kisser Jeff," Jackie said to me with a look of disgust on her face. From that moment forward I despised her. *What a bitch*! My prepubescent self thought at the time. I was already insecure about being knee-deep in my ugly stage. Curly and nappy blowdried hair with braces and a few zits. Exactly who I'm sure Jackie envisioned. And now I messed up the kissing part, too. Nice going Jeff....

When Brian and Jason invited me to play spin-the-bottle with two eighth graders—Jackie and Michelle—I was in heaven. My first kiss was going to be with one of two older, and likely very experienced, pretty girls. My imagination went wild with what kind of action they must've had. I didn't really know them, but I certainly knew *who* they were. Every boy in school had a crush on them. Especially Jackie. Jackie walked the halls with a certain confidence that just made you crave her even more. Long, red hair. Alluring, bright green eyes. Almost as if she wore colored contacts, except they hadn't been invented yet. Perfect lips. A smile that made you feel good. Just enough freckles to dazzle you. And Michelle, well, her boobs had developed more quickly than the other thirteen-year-old girls, so it was hard for her to go unnoticed by anyone at Yorktown Middle School. Sure, she had nice oval brown eyes, and wavy black hair and all that, but all the boys lusted over Michelle's biggest-in-class breasts. Other than the *Oui* and *Playboy* magazines I illegally bought from Steve down the street at four times the cover price, I really hadn't thought much about boobs until encountering Michelle. Michelle was nice, too. Almost like she didn't know how pretty she was.

I never imagined in my wildest dreams that I'd be lucky enough to have these girls as my first two kisses. I figured I'd have to settle for seventh graders Rachel or Sandy. Semi-cute, but certainly not Jackie caliber. I had sent a note to Sandy the week before:

"Will you go out with me? Check the box yes or no."

Sandy had just emerged from her awkward braces and pimple stage too, so as I'd suspected, she checked yes. Up until that point, neither of us had great options in terms of boyfriends and girlfriends, but at least I made her laugh. Other than meeting at the mall once, nothing ever happened with Sandy.

I was determined to never speak to Jackie again. Just because she was the pretty girl in school and I was the ugly duckling didn't give her the right to treat me with such disdain simply because I sucked at kissing. I guess it was better than if she had outright refused to kiss me despite my lucky spin on the empty plastic two-liter Diet Rite bottle. Still, I was furious and embarrassed. Over the next eight years, I attended high school and college with Jackie. Even though I was no longer thinking about her shove and admonishment from 1982, I had no desire to befriend her. So not once in high school or college did we ever speak. Not even a hello on the street at Ohio State or in the hallways of Walnut Ridge High School. Intentional or not, we didn't even make eye contact all those years.

It took a couple years since my Jackie experience to no longer be the ugly kid in school. Girls eventually started paying a little attention to me. And that is when I met my first real girlfriend, Kim. I got to exchange a few real kisses in the intervening two years, but no full extended make-out sessions until Kim. That was about to change. On May 13, 1985, in my mom's five-speed blue Subaru hatchback, Kim and I shared our first kiss. Or should I say, forty minutes of making out. It was only a few minutes into our kiss that Kim took a step back, looked me in the eye, and told me, "You are by far the best kisser I've ever met!" Not gonna lie, after Jackie, I knew that I needed to change my style. I had to do the opposite of what I had seen on TV. *Days of Our Lives* could no longer be the benchmark for romance. So, thanks to Jackie, I became the softest, most fully aware and sensual kisser known to boy-kind. No way in hell was I going to be shoved and accused of animalistic tendencies again.

That might be the end of a nice story of how I became a good kisser, but in 2010, Jackie, about forty-one years old, sent me a request on Facebook. I obviously wasn't angry anymore, but it was a bit odd. I knew nothing about Jackie. We hadn't spoken in decades. Before I accepted her request, I sent her a message:

"Wanna hear a funny story?"

Jackie and I spoke on the phone and I told her the nasty Jackie story I had lived with for over thirty years.

"That's hilarious, Jeff! I remember that day well. You see, you were my first kiss and I thought I had totally screwed up. I had no idea what to do. I totally freaked out and instead of crying, I blamed it all on you. But I knew it was my fault."

All these years, and it turns out Jackie was just another scared kid like me. No clue what she was doing! Avoiding embarrassment in front of three teenage boys and her friend Michelle. She wasn't the nasty tough girl I had created in my head all those years.

"Weren't you totally grossed out, though, to be kissing an ugly boy like me?"

"Oh my god, Jeff, no way. I thought you were totally cute."

We both laughed. All these years and Jackie wasn't a mean girl after all. She even thought I was marginally cute, or she was blind, or maybe she was just being nice. If I only knew then what I know now. Today, Jackie is a chef and has an amazing cookbook on the market. I bought the book the second it hit the shelves. As for Michelle, we connected after both of our divorces and dated for a couple months, and I had plenty of practice by this time around. Plus, I got to do more than kiss her finally. Jackie and Michelle both turned out to be great people.

5

Walking on Water

"Tatty, is it true that Christians really believe that Jesus walked on water? Sounds silly if you ask me!"

Asher was just seven when he asked me this question in a that's-just-absurd tone. *Tatty* is Yiddish for father, and that's what my kids have always called me since I speak a fair amount of Yiddish and thought of Tatty as more affectionate than just *Dad*.

I always tried to teach my kids to respect people of all religions and cultures. This was one of those moments of truth. Asher wasn't the type to naturally judge others, but he clearly was developing ideas about others' beliefs that could lead him in the wrong direction. Do I tell him, "Yeah, we Jews don't believe that paranormal nonsense" and undo the respect I had demanded of him since he was old enough to talk? Or was now the time to come up with a more creative plan to preserve his organic love and respect of others? I had left the world of religious Judaism a year earlier and still had some sour feelings, so I easily could have just blasted all religion. I paused to think about what I wanted to say and made my decision.

"Asher, is it true Jews really believe that two of every animal from Alaska to Australia hopped on one boat in perfect cooperation with Noah?" I told him in a chew-on-this voice. "Or how about a talking snake in the Garden of Eden?" Asher had been attending Jewish school since kindergarten and was told by his bearded teachers that all the stories in the Torah, the Old Testament, were true. "You see, Asher, all religions have lots of stories that don't match logical science, so let's be careful before we throw stones at others' beliefs." He understood right away.

Fifteen years prior, while in law school, a man in a black hat with a foot-long graying beard approached me in the Jewish Law Students Association office at the University of Toledo. He was one of those Chassidic Jews in, of all places, Ohio. "I'm trying to get a Gemurah class together. Any of you guys want to join?" he asked four of us. "A Ge-what?" I inquired of the ultra-Orthodox rabbi. "Oh, Gemurah. That's the Talmud. A collection of legal debates over what Jewish law says on a whole host of issues." I had heard of the word Talmud before, but I still didn't take the bait. "Thanks, but no thanks, Rabbi. I have enough legal stuff to study in law school. The last thing I want is to add to that." Clearly sensing my apprehension with religion and his scraggly beard and long black coat, the rabbi gently pulled me aside. "How about we just study the Jewish views on happiness, sadness, joy, and despair? You know, the human condition."

Growing up in a liberal, mostly non-religious Jewish home, I had no idea there was a Jewish view on any of those things. A part of me was scared to enter or even take a peek into his world, but another part of me was curious why after twenty-three years I had no idea what Judaism had to say about anything other than the Holocaust. I knew more names of death camps than I knew books of the Bible. A week later, my spiritual journey began. For the next six months, I devoured Jewish texts on human behavior. On love. Anger. Rejoicing. Depression. It was fascinating, and for the first time in my life, I was ready to accept that there might be a higher power. That Judaism was authentic. What made it even easier was that Rabbi Shemtov and his family practiced love and kindness day in and day out. It was contagious. "You can bring on that Gemurah thing now, Rabbi," I recall telling him after months of learning. I quickly became a part of the rabbi's loving family.

Then came Rosh Hashanah 1993. My second year of law school. I was going to celebrate the first Jewish new year as a believer of sorts. "Jeffrey, today we celebrate 5,753 years since God created the world," the rabbi excitedly explained. "What do you mean?" I responded without much pause. Maybe he was half-joking. "The earth is billions of years old. Dinosaurs are hundreds of millions of years old. They have the bones to prove it," I reminded him just in case he was serious. I was never one to just accept something without some level of proof. A natural thinker. I already made the leap to believe in an unproven invisible God, but now I was supposed to believe the earth was less than six thousand years old? "There may be proof of dinosaur bones, but not that dinosaurs ever walked the planet," Rabbi Shemtov said in an overly confident tone. "Could it be that God put the bones here to challenge us, to think about whether to believe in his word or not?" he asked me. You heard me right. Rabbi Shemtov, as kind as he was, really believed that the bones were put here by God so Jews would have to try really hard to either believe the literal words of the Bible or believe in that gobblygook science stuff.

I had never considered that prehistoric bones may have been created by God any more than whether the earth was flat or round. Didn't even occur to me. But Rabbi Shemtov wasn't budging. "And when God made this world, isn't it possible he made the world in an already aged state? If God created a full grown tree today, and we measured the tree's life at that full grown state, wouldn't it register that the tree was maybe a hundred years old, even though we know the tree really was only created now?" I was silenced into thinking to myself. The rabbi had challenged everything I had ever accepted about science. And some of it made sense. At least at the time. Or maybe I just wanted to believe that there was purpose to everything in life after years of learning about the slaughter of the Jews. "But what about evolution, Rabbi?" Rabbi Shemtov still didn't waiver in his quick response. "Isn't it possible that God made many monkeys and pre-humanlike creatures before creating the first man, Adam? Creatures without human souls?" I guess so, I thought to myself, but the Darwin ape charts seemed so convincing in elementary school. I hadn't even caught that Rabbi Shemtov said monkeys instead of apes, really showing off his ignorance on the subject. Since I already had accepted the authenticity of Judaism, I didn't put up a bigger fight and half-accepted what Rabbi Shemtov told me, even many years later trying to convince family members that the science we knew and loved was sometimes warped. I left the subject alone for the next few years. It was easier to avoid the topic while I focused on the more spiritual aspects of my learning.

I was a sponge for Jewish religious knowledge. I read and learned and studied. I read more Jewish texts than my law school books. I learned in English, Hebrew, and Yiddish. Week in and week out, I digested Jewish text after text, until I came across a book by one of the most respected and revered Jewish leaders of all time, Maimonides. Maimonides, also known as Rambam (an acronym for his name, Moses Ben Maimon), lived in twelfth-century Egypt. He was a physician, and to this day is still considered one of the seminal Jewish thinkers of all time, on the same level in stature as Aristotle and Socrates in philosophy. Maimonides wrote numerous volumes of works, but one that caught my eye was called *The Guide for the Perplexed*. I read the complicated book from cover to cover in two days. Even read a chapter during my Torts class in law school. Then I read it again. It seemed to contradict most of what Rabbi Shemtov had taught me about science. That the world was not literally created in seven days, but rather each "day" might represent millions if not billions of years. That the earth was not literally six thousand years old. That some of the stories in the Bible could be allegorical. Now, there's a thought.

"Rabbi, I thought Maimonides was a giant on Jewish thought. Why is he saying all these things that contradict many ideas you taught me about creation?" "Jeffrey, the book is called The Guide for the *Perplexed*," he said while drawing out and emphasizing the word perplexed. "If you're not perplexed, you're not supposed to read the book. It's for a different audience than someone like you who isn't perplexed." Without further discussion, I blindly accepted his explanation and reverted back to the literalism I had been taught to follow. I was officially brainwashed. It no longer mattered whether the answers to my questions made sense. I had stopped using my God-given lawyer skills and started taking on sheeplike qualities. *Baaaaahhhh.*

I carried that literalism with me into the real world after law school. I left Ohio and moved to St. Louis. Joined a prestigious law firm. Got married. Had kids. Started raising a family. All the while believing that the earth was created in seven days, that Noah's Ark really hosted pairs of every animal on the planet on one big-ass boat, that humans really started with one human being, and so on. When I needed "answers," there were plenty of teachers and rabbis to provide what I needed. The "proofs" fit my narrative. I had bought into the literalism hook, line and sinker, and I was prepared to defend it to the most logical of foes. My brain depletion was complete.

Within three short years, I had convinced my father, new wife and others that everything ever said in the Bible and scores of other Jewish texts were literally true, all commanded by God at Mount Sinai under a thundering sky. That God even gave us countless Jewish rules on technology that hadn't been invented three thousand years ago.

I may have stayed sucked into the abyss of this logic-less life had it not been for the dysfunction I was about to witness in the world of Orthodox Judaism.

Where to even begin.

"Can I ask you a legal question," Rabbi Goldstein asked me right after a weeknight prayer service one cold winter night in 1998. "Sure," I responded as if he was about to inquire about his rights as a tenant or ask about some constitutional issue in the news. Maybe about abortion or prayer in school. Instead, Rabbi Goldstein wanted to embark on some complicated real estate tax scheme to funnel money to one of the Orthodox Jewish schools, profit from business deals, and avoid paying the government any taxes, all while making a pretty penny for himself. "You can't tell anyone what I am about to ask you," he continued. After listening to him without interruption for the next few minutes, I didn't want to hear anymore. "You know what, Rabbi, this is way out of my area of expertise. You'll have to ask someone else. Sorry." I was only three years out of law school, so it was an easy out. I had read newspaper articles about fraudulent schemes to raise money for some of the more extreme Chassidic schools in New York, even read an article about some Chassidic rabbis in Brooklyn arrested for dealing drugs to make money for their schools. But St. Louis, too? I never told a soul.

Two years later, after the morning prayer services at synagogue, a shouting match broke out among two ultra-Orthodox men. It was over one divorced man's attempt to get romantic with a single woman in the community. Two consenting adults interested in each other. Before I could figure out the details, Mordechai clocked Yaacov straight in the face with his clenched fist. He fell to the ground with blood pouring from the side of his eye. Mordechai just shouted, "Talk to her again and the next time I won't be so nice." Then he spit on Yaacov's face as he lie on the ground in pain and shock. I was stunned. These "Godly" men were resorting to violence? I left for work in disgust but said nothing.

It was pretty common for Orthodox Jews to have other Orthodox Jews over for massive carb-filled meals every Friday night for dinner and Saturday lunch after prayers at the synagogue. A typical meal might consist of one course with fish and four to five different sugar-filled mayo inspired salads, a second course of soup, a third course with chicken, beef, and some other meat-stuffed doughy entrée, two or three potato or sugar-filled kugels, a vegetable usually covered with a sauce laced with sugar, then desserts. Lots and lots of desserts. Cookies, pies, cakes, and maybe some dairy-free ice cream. All in all, a lunch might offer up the chance at three thousand plus calories and a hundred fifty grams of sugar per person. The comraderie aspect is unparalleled in any other commuity, but the health part, not so much.

One day, our family was invited to the Berenfeld house for lunch. We sat down, said the prayer over sweet grape wine, ate some challah (oops, I forgot about this sugared-up, Jewish sweet egg bread), and then started the meal. Before Yonaton passed the fish to me, he started up with thoughts all too common in ultra-Orthodox circles. "I was so conflicted today on my walk back from *shul*." Shul is Yiddish for synagogue. "A woman riding her bike passed me and wished me a good *Shabbos*. On the one hand, it was sort of nice, but on the other, she was violating Shabbos so it didn't feel that great." Shabbos is the Yiddish word for the Jewish Sabbath where Orthodox Jews refrain from a whole host of activities, including driving, riding bikes and the like. So a woman, probably Jewish herself but not Orthodox, was riding her bike and took time to give her side-curls sporting Jewish neighbor a friendly Sabbath greeting. Instead of appreciating the gesture, Yonaton was too busy judging her violations of God's holy laws. I lost my appetite, which probably was the healthy choice anyway.

In 2004, Missourians took to the polls to vote on whether gay marriage should be banned under the state's constitution. Missouri is a pretty conservative state, so I assumed the amendment would pass, but when signs supporting the ban popped up on a couple dozen lawns of my co-religionists, I wanted to puke. On my friend Yisroel's lawn, one read "BAN GAY MARRIAGE! GOD SAYS SO!" "Yisroel, why do you need to put a sign up on your lawn? You could have a neighbor who is gay and that could make him or her feel really bad." "It's an *avera*, Jeffrey. Plain and simple." Avera is Hebrew for sin. Yisroel didn't seem to care about whether a gay person's feelings would be harmed. "So of all the issues in the world… Poverty. Racism. Hunger. You think gay marriage is the pressing issue?" What really got him was when I half-jokingly reminded him that while the rest of the world was getting divorced, bad-mouthing marriage, or experiencing mental or physical spousal abuse, gays were the one group that still was pro-marriage.

They desperately wanted so bad to be able to marry their partners. "Maybe we could learn something from that," I sarcastically remarked. Ironically, the divorce rate among Orthodox Jews in our community was surprisingly high.

My discomfort with the community continued to build each day, but I told no one, internalizing all that stress. Most of the time I let pass without comment the weekly disturbances.

"Did you see those *shfartzas* walking down Delmar Boulevard earlier," Shmuel Katz asked me one Friday night walking back from synagogue, in a *beware of them* kind of way. Shfartza literally means black in Yiddish, but it is used by religious Jews in a derogatory way, much like the *N* word is used in English. This was where I mentally took a U-turn after years of sweeping weekly shfartza comments from scores of Orthodox Jews under the rug. Shmuel was one of the pillars of the community. Widely respected in religious circles. A successful business man, too. If even he was part of the dysfunction, if even he was racist, was there any hope at all?

"Why are you racist?" I asked in my most direct tone despite usually letting these comments go. "I'm not racist," he quickly responded as if that would address what just came out of his self-declared religious mouth. "Let me ask you, Shmuel… if Rav Shach was here with us right now, would you have said the word schfartza in front of him?" Rav is short-handed Hebrew for Rabbi. "Probably not," Shmuel admitted. "Well," I continued, "I know an even bigger rabbi you shouldn't say it in front of." Rabbi Shach to most black-hat wearing Jews was the most revered rabbi in all the world. Despite living in B'nei Brak, Israel, one of the most extreme Jewish religious communities in the world, and having almost no contact with the rest of humanity, Rabbi Shach instructed Jews worldwide on just about every issue. He was the Pope for these Jews. If

Rabbi Shach said jump, ultra-religious Jews would jump and jump and jump until the rabbi said to stop. To many, it was like God himself was speaking. "So there is this rabbi I know who knows your every thought and hears your every word," I told Shmuel in a baiting tone. "Who are you talking about," Shmuel asked curiously, as if I was about to introduce him to an amazing rabbi. "His name is God," I said in a scolding voice. "He knows what you're thinking and hears every word uttered by you. So if you wouldn't say *schfartza* in front of Rabbi Shach, you certainly shouldn't say it in front of God. Or even think it." I felt free for a moment. Shmuel looked at me with remorse on his face and for the first time in my ten years in the world of Orthodox Judaism, someone owned up to the racism. "I have a problem, Jeffrey. I'm racist. I need to work on it." We walked silently the rest of the way home.

If you think blacks were disparaged in the Orthodox community, Arabs got it much worse. Kids as young as six were often heard telling jokes about Arabs. Adults, even doctors, suggested carpet-bombing entire countries in the Middle East. Anti-Arab and anti-Muslim ideas flowed off the tongues of so many on a regular basis. All, of course, justified because Israel is under siege by all one billion Muslims. At least that's what they were led to believe.

These situations repeated themselves over and over in a variety of forms over the ensuing several years, and I finally had enough. I wasn't wired to handle xenophobia or rigidity. My DNA was programmed to love and respect people of all backgrounds and beliefs. I eventually got divorced and walked away from the trauma of the religious world. For the first time in a long time, I was enjoying life again. After finally leaving Orthodoxy years after the schfartza incidents, I quickly was able to regain my brain. My ability to use common sense. To think. To not accept ridiculous ideas in the name of religion. To be proud of my deep Jewish heritage while remaining true to the greatness of humanity and respect of others, ideas ironically that are promoted in many Jewish religious texts. To stay true to the main principle of my heritage, to love one fellow as one loves himself, all while many Orthodox Jews translate loving one's fellow to mean only loving one's fellow Jews. The funny thing is that the word "Jew" appears nowhere in that "love your fellow" commandment in the Bible.

Most Jews aren't Orthodox, and certainly not all Orthodox Jews are xenophobic or reject science, but I finally found my way back to a Jewish spirituality that appreciates the depth of Judaism while also appreciating the colorful diversity our world has to offer. My friends today include people named Yaacov and Shmuel, and Mohammed, Adnan, and Amir. Robert and William. They include all stripes of Jews, Christians, Muslims, and others. Gay and straight. All created in the real image of God. At least according to Judaism.

6

Have a seat right here on the couch

I'm a little angry—okay more than a little—that seeing a therapist was considered a bit taboo in the 1980s and 90s. I remember when I met my girlfriend Lisa during law school in 1994, she was knee deep in therapy. Once a week, like clockwork, she saw a middle-aged social worker, Joan.

"You see a what?" I asked her in my immature, twenty-five-year-old tone. "Why do you need to pay someone to talk to you? Can't you just work it out yourself?"

Don't judge my un-evolved self too harshly. After all, everyone called psychologists "shrinks" back then, and people in therapy were often just chalked up as crazy. At least that's what I thought of them. Vice presidential candidate Tom Eagleton of Missouri once got electric shock therapy for depression in the 1970s and it cost George McGovern the election. Instead we got Richard Nixon, all because society wasn't mature enough to handle someone addressing their shit. Weird thing is I worked in the same law firm as Senator Eagleton when I got out of law school. I'll tell you my stories of him another time.

I later learned that Lisa was molested by her grandfather when she was nine years old. I didn't know about it at the time, but I'm pretty sure that's not something you just "work out yourself!" She wasn't crazy. Wasn't feeble. Just in need of serious healing. And only the kind that could come from years and years of professional help.

I really hadn't thought much about my own sometimes fucked up childhood back then. Or really any time until recently. I worked three jobs to pay for college, attended law school on a full ride and became a successful lawyer. I'm raising three amazing kids and love being a soft caring dad. I've made amazing friends over the years. Really deep friendships with some amazing men. I'm active civically. Yada yada yada. It never dawned on me that I had any lingering issues from my own childhood trauma. Life, while not perfect, was pretty damn good. I knew firsthand of my family's severe financial struggles, my father's infidelity and all of the yelling, incessant I'm-leaving-you frying pan throwing, wall punches and the like, but I just hadn't thought it affected me all that much. In my mind, I made it—*despite* that shit. Plus, I knew my parents loved me despite all of our family shit. Maybe it was wishful thinking, but I was thoroughly convinced I beat the odds. Someone else in my shoes easily could've turned to substance abuse or given up on life. Or remained financially challenged. Not me. I was impervious to everything they threw at me. So I thought.

Then came Rebecca.

Rebecca was beautiful. She was deep. Highly intelligent. So spiritual in a way I had never seen in a woman. She believed in and worked on growth. A smile that lit up a room. Had a wicked sense of humor and a cackling, hilarious laugh to match. She understood the importance of intimacy. She craved new information despite already knowing a lot about people and the world. Even was self-aware enough to admit when she was wrong. Okay, maybe only occasionally. Still, was this a fantasy? Was she real?

We started to date. Well, sort of. She wasn't truly ready for a relationship, having just endured a horrific breakup a mere three weeks before we met. Yet she still wanted to be a huge part of my life and see me several days a week. We spent six months together under the guise of this undefined, half-ass, not dating, but in a sometimes sexual, sometimes friends, sometimes not speaking to each other, sometimes dating dynamic. Not exactly a dream relationship.

Despite all of Rebecca's greatness, she had her own problems. She was avoidant. Too guarded to get super close. Sometimes unaffectionate. She would often be insulting, critical, and downright mean. While she maintained this all had to do with her own recent and painful breakup with another man, I only ever knew that distant and easily annoyed version of her. I never got to know the Rebecca-proclaimed kind, loving, affectionate woman. Her lack of consistent connection sent me into the worst emotional tailspins of my life, always begging for her attention and affection but rarely getting it. I found myself looking at my phone constantly, hoping she would text. Or call. Anything. I used to check to see when she logged onto social media in the morning so I knew when she was awake, then I would sit by the phone and hope she texted me a good morning. Nothing most of the time. Would this be a day she held my hand or kissed me? Or would she for the hundredth time tell me I couldn't touch her, like when she refused to kiss me on her birthday after I dropped off flowers, with nothing to say to me other than that they were too expensive. Would I get a welcoming hug or a dispassionate "Hey, what's up?" Would she tell me she loves me, or pretend we were just pals? Every day I was on eggshells hoping for something that wasn't there. She would even unintentionally tease me by telling me she was now ready to actually be in a real relationship with me, that she was deeply in love with me… only to back off three days, a week, or in the best scenario, two weeks later. "Sorry, I need more healing," was her mantra each time.

I felt so insecure. So worthless. Downright shameful at times. Rebecca even had the *chutzpah* to blame a lot of our dynamic on me, suggesting two weeks after I met her that I see a therapist.

"You have serious attachment issues, Jeffrey. You need therapy," she said in her all familiar, unloving stoic way. Rebecca had seen therapists off and on for three decades and had become a little too "expert" on the subject of psychology. This was right after she told me I needed to lose weight, too.

But like many of her blunt statements, she made me think about myself. Not to blame myself for her nastiness, coldness or distance, or her inability to be in a consistent relationship. That's on her, healing or not. Yet I still wanted to know. Did I really have these attachment issues? I had never even heard of the term. I thought attachment was a piece you put on a vacuum cleaner hose. The question remained, though. Did I need serious help? How could that be. I had conquered so many challenges in life all on my own. I worked my way out of a family in constant economic peril. I became a soft, loving dad unlike my own sometimes absent one who was too busy screwing other women to be home for dinner. Except for once in a relationship that was over many months before the official breakup, I remained a loyal partner to almost everyone I dated, despite my dad's habitual wandering eye. And wandering hands. I had the most caring and loving friends a person could ask for. So why did I need help?

Mostly because I wanted so bad for things with Rebecca to work out, I signed up for the stupid therapy she suggested. The same reason I ate a healthier diet and upped my exercise. Because Rebecca said I was in bad shape, and I needed to fix that. I did it all, too. To please her. At least initially.

I had seen a therapist a grand total of two sessions during my divorce twelve years prior. Dr. Cohen. He was the leading expert in St. Louis on the impact of divorce on children. I was scared stiff that leaving my wife would be bad for my kids that I had enough sense to seek help on the topic. When I learned that my kids' emotional health wouldn't come down to whether I was married to their mom, but instead to how well we co-parented, I knew it was safe to get divorced. I took his advice and have cooperated with their mom ever since. I then saw a therapist for maybe three sessions after a broken engagement seven years later. I learned a little why I was picking certain unaffectionate women as partners, which was helpful, but no major childhood trauma breakthroughs.

This time was different. Within a few sessions with my therapist, she identified that I indeed had suffered tremendously from my childhood. From the constant arguing, the infidelity I discovered as an eleven-year-old boy but told no one, the threats of divorce my parents exchanged each week. The phone line and electricity being shut off because my parents seomtimes couldn't afford to pay the bills. Insecurity, both financially and emotionally, was the norm in my childhood. The therapist was in agreement with Rebecca on one thing.

I had attachment issues, and the good news is she said we could fix it! Just identifying the problem and knowing I could conquer it was like a mountain lifted from my unknowing, long-burdened shoulders.

As a result of years of unaddressed childhood trauma, I apparently had played out that insecurity and longing for attachment in my personal life, mainly in my relationships with women. In virtually every relationship with women I had dated since high school, save two, I felt highly insecure and found myself begging for attention and affection, even when I was getting a healthy amount. To make matters worse, I was still choosing less affectionate people, probably as a source of familiarity. Although certainly not the comforting kind. My childhood trauma was in charge and I was never let in on that not-so-small detail.

Early on, Rebecca had said something that didn't initially sit right with me. That everything happens for some cosmic, good reason, whether to achieve greatness or to correct something in a person. Or some other reason. I didn't completely buy that philosophy then because I've always had a tough time understanding why bad things happen to good people, but I certainly know now at least one reason why she entered my life. For the correction of my own severely damaged soul.

It is ironic, then, that Rebecca, the queen trigger of my worst insecurities and attachment, suggested therapy! How dare the person who made me feel the most alone in my life tell me about therapy because I wanted her attention. But alas, she was right, as she was about a gazillion other things.

Five months of therapy later, after decades of breathing in the polluted air of my childhood, I finally am recognizing and managing my attachment issues. I feel stronger. More equipped. Healthier each week. My stomach hurts less. I itch less. I'm learning to ride out an unhealthy feeling creeping into my unsuspecting conscious, rather than act it out in negative behavior. Instead of mimicking the eleven-year-old boy who saw his world come crashing down, I'm being an adult. My road still has a few twists and turns and maybe even some lane-changing bumps along the way, but at least I have GPS this time. Plus, I have a brand-new, healthy and fit body to navigate my childhood obstacle course, also courtesy of Rebecca. Ok. Ok. I had something to do with it, too.

Thanks in a now-I-know-why-you-were-sent-to-me kind of way for getting me to face my trauma. And thanks for calling me fat, Rebecca.

You were right as usual. Things do seem to happen for a higher reason.

7

Rebecca's Kaleidoscope

You have the depth of the Mariana Trench
Humor of a hyena. Laughing. Laughing. Laughing. Deep
cackling belly laughs

You anger like Katrina crashing on the shores of an already
poor community, as if that doesn't matter. And sometimes
you create the distance of the Darién Gap

Your beauty rivals the Cliffs of Moher
Longing with the heart of the Asiatic lion

Wrath like a thousand suns
with your sometime sadness of Jeanne d'Arc

Yet you grow and grow and grow, as if a strong Baobab tree,
living for hundreds of years

Intelligence of vos Savant
But you tantrum like a summer storm

and cover with the coldness of Verkhoyansk
Then you shine, more than the light of Venus in a late
September sky

The brilliance of the roundest diamond
Your claws of the harpy eagle hurt so much
with the itchiness of hogweed

But then your wisdom reaches beyond the Oracle of Delphi
Something so special about you, as if you were the first child
born to a new mother

Bitter as the taste of white dandelions
sometimes sharp like Cutco. *Ouch!*

You emerge, though, loving as the Aries zodiac
faithful as the yellow crested penguin

Analytical as Curie
and as judging as one of seventy-one in the Sanhedrin

Affectionate and touching. Sensual
Amazing, alluring as a Windsor Beauty

Pain of a first degree burn
The trauma of a broken heart, that has been with you so long

8

Lions, Spiders, and Snakes, Oh My!

I didn't fully appreciate what I had signed up for. A midnight trek in the rainforest in Costa Rica sounded adventurous. I was told that different animals come out at night and there would be an opportunity to see a lot of cool things. Having only been to zoos previously, it hadn't dawned on me that there wouldn't be cages or bars. No rivers or embankments between us and the animals. To add insult to injury, the phrase "rainy season," also hadn't sunk in. In my mind, I was going to see an exhibit of some sort, albeit at night.

"Be here at eleven thirty tonight," the sixty-something -year-old, hippie-looking woman with gray and black hair braids at the excursion counter told us after we paid fifty dollars for the so-called hike. "Then a van will take the group to the starting point. You're going to absolutely love this," she said as she gave us a reassuring smile.

It was only two in the afternoon, so I didn't give the night-time hike much more thought as we went about our day. I was in Costa Rica with Lori and we were halfway broken up before the trip even began, so I was trying to fill my day with fun things that allowed me to stay distracted. Lori was a few years older than me, forty-five at the time, and had never been married. Exceptionally kind and compassionate in her non-romantic personal life, but a bit critical in romantic relationships. It didn't help that we were both emotional and I hadn't worked through my childhood trauma yet, either. I decided to take a nap around eight o'clock so I wasn't completely exhausted for the two hour midnight hike. Plus, that would take up another few hours without having to interact with Lori.

We arrived fifteen minutes early to catch the van to the hiking area. There were only six other people on the van, plus the guide, who looked like he just walked out of the Crocodile Dundee movie, Australian hat and all. He was fifty something, about five-foot eleven, and semi-muscular but with a protruding belly. His face looked like it had been through wars, tsunamis, and the desert. It was distinguished, yet worn. His hair was a yellowish blond that stuck out through the sides of his beige, canvas-leather hat.

"Howdy everyone!" he greeted us on the van.

My first thought was, *Howdy? Really?* Was this necessary? Did I just sign up for a Disney adventure? Was he going to start singing "It's a small world after all?"

"Tonight is going to be spectacular," he continued. "How many people here have hiked in the dark?" Not surprisingly, nobody raised their hand. He went on and on about the wildlife that only comes out at night and how we might see this animal or that. It started to rain lightly outside. He passed out high-powered flashlights and instructed all eight of us to wrap the straps around our wrists so we didn't lose them.

"Okay, ladies and gents. Here we are."

I looked around for a trailhead or some semblance of a path, but there was nothing. Just dense forest. The rain started coming down harder and faster.

"Everyone, put on your raincoats. This is going to be a wet night!" he told us with a chuckle and smile. I didn't find it all that inviting, but we were here so what the hell.

"Stay single file behind me and don't veer off to the side of where I'm walking."

We started into the forest with nothing but brush and trees ahead of us. After about five minutes of walking through the now pouring rain and listening to haunting thunder, Dundee got excited. "Check this out! You're going to love this." He shined his flashlight onto a fallen tree trunk as we all looked at a tarantula the size of a flattened grapefruit. "What a beauty!" he smiled again.

I never really put beauty and spiders in the same category, but it was cool looking, from my ten-foot distance. He showed us another twenty species of spiders and bugs along the next ten minutes of our hike. I began to wonder if this is what he meant by "all these animals that only come out at night." I didn't realize I signed up for the bug tour.

Then it happened.

From the tops of the trees, some form of monkey or ape started screaming, howling and growling at high pitches. I flashed my light into the air, trying to find out what was happening. We were under attack. At least that's what it sounded like. Was I about to die? One twenty-year-old college girl started to scream she was so scared. "I want to go home!" she told her boyfriend.

"Everyone calm down," our guide said laughing. "These are howler monkeys. They aren't going to hurt us. They just are letting us know this is their territory and we aren't to disturb it. Look! You can see one up there," as he flashed his light in the corner of a short tree. None of us saw the monkey. "Let's continue walking."

The rain had gotten so intense you could barely see a foot in front of you. The ground had become swampy, and our feet sunk into the ground as we proceeded through the dense jungle. Yes, jungle. I couldn't think of it as a forest anymore given our encounter with the monkeys.

I looked at my watch. We had been hiking for almost an hour and a half. Finally, the hike was coming to an end. At least that's what I thought, until our guide said, "Holy shit! Everyone slowly walk backwards twenty steps." I tried to look around the four people in front of me but had no idea what was going on. We had reversed course for about twenty steps when he finally told us. "Look very carefully where I point my flash light." None of us could see anything. "Right there," he pointed. Then it moved. A massive black and brown snake, blending in with the trees around it, slivered in the opposite direction. "That, my friends, is a fer-de-lance viper snake. One bite from that snake and you're a goner. Maybe five minutes to live," he smiled wide, confusing us about whether he was joking or not.

Are you fucking serious? I had just paid for a hike to come within ten feet of a deadly poisonous snake? For some reason, they left that part out of the brochure. It didn't seem to fit in well with the "you're gonna love this hike" crap they told us when paying.

After another fifteen minutes, we exited the jungle to an open road where our van was waiting for us. I was the first to get on. A part of me felt accomplished. A survivor. A real renaissance man. But then there was the part of me that was in shock that I ever agreed to go hiking through the pouring rain in the pitch black night to look at spiders and snakes. Lori didn't seem so bad after all.

9

Jack

Home run!! I was a righty, but I still clobbered the ball to right field, straight over our neighbor's chest-high wire fence and into the yard where Cliff the Doberman Pincher resided. I was lucky enough to hit the ball that hard off Jimmy's fastball. Fortunately, being the older brother, I made Michael climb the fence to retrieve the ball while a few neighborhood kids and I distracted the vicious dog at the other end of the fence. Aaron and I already had been playing baseball in our backyard for several years when the Simersons moved in. I don't remember who was there before, but I know there was no boy-eating dog. We really didn't know the Simersons, but oh did we know about their menacing black Doberman. Cliff looked at us like we were dessert! We were the only Jews on the block, and Dad didn't exactly alleviate our fears by telling us the Germans used Doberman pinchers in the Holocaust against the Jews. We already were told never to buy a BMW, but now we had to hate dogs because of the Nazi past, too? Dad could barely afford our used two-door Caucasian-flesh colored compact Datsun 210 so

I'm not sure why we were discussing Beemers. I never really pictured Germans or their dogs with names like Cliff anyway. Had the dog's name been Adolphus, Otto or Heinrich, I would've accepted Dad's condemnation without pause. My own kids have a German Sheppard at their mom's house now, and she certainly seems to love us Jews just fine. I get dog slobber on my face when I pick them up to prove it.

In fairness to Cliff, my fear of dogs dated back long before the Simersons moved next door. Mom and Dad couldn't afford a dog, so my brother Michael and I already had a natural fear of them. So much so that in the third grade, a twenty-five pound brown and white French Bulldog, with his flattened, wrinkled face, came running into the street while I was about halfway on my bike ride to Old Orchard Elementary. The only thing I knew about bulldogs is that they were the featured mean dogs in *Tom & Jerry* cartoons. So mean they had to be kept on a chain in a dog house located in the backyard. Menacing to Tom the cat. Barking and growling. And now that same type of dog was after me. I slammed the brakes on my used Mongoose dirt bike, made mostly of spare parts my friend Kenny gave me. The little Frenchie circled my bike for twenty minutes, growling and snorting as though he was planning an attack. I cried hysterically during his entire stakeout. "I WANT MY MOMMY!"

Finally, when the little dog waddled off to pee, I mustered every ounce of courage to escape. I never saw him again. I should've known better than to take Brice Road to school. It was much quicker than riding down Balsam Road or Portsmouth Drive, but a Great Dane the size of a small horse had once barked at me from behind his tall fence months earlier on this route so it served me right going that way. Too risky. The Great Dane was bigger than the Shetland ponies shown in the "Smallest Horse in the World" booths at the Ohio State Fair.

It was probably a good thing we didn't have money for a pet aside from the occasional Ziploc bagged tadpole or gold fish won at our synagogue's annual Purim carnival, each of which usually ended up flushed down the toilet after premature deaths. It wasn't that hard to win them as prizes. Simply toss a pingpong ball into a sea of gold fish bowls and if it lands in one, you are now the proud owner of a fish with a usually one-month death sentence. I must have gone through a half dozen goldfish between third and seventh grade. Tadpole Billy lasted the longest. Two months after joining our family, he got an eye infection and it eventually bursted in the water, killing him instantly. Michael and I saw the whole thing in horror right before our eyes. Billy had two legs forming, on his way to becoming a real animal, so that death hit me a little harder than the others.

Not having pets wasn't just the cause of my fear of dogs, but it also made me less sensitive to animals. In 1981, I used my paper route money and bought a beta fish, you know those kinds that don't get along with other beta fish. I always thought of this species as a metaphor for how some humans act. Aaron and I used to take a mirror to the side of the fish bowl and watch Henrietta blow up in anger after seeing her reflection. I thought she was going to have a fishy heart attack. We had enough sense not to make her stare for too long. We were *bad*, but not that bad.

It's a good thing we didn't have any pets. Our house was such a pig sty that any uncaged animal likely would've landed us a visit from the Columbus Department of Social Services. Paperwork and clutter everywhere. Brown goop between the bathroom tiles in the shower. Dirty dishes stacked high, even after Dad bought our first dishwasher that we had to roll over to the sink and hook up with a hose. For years I was embarrassed to have friends over, until I finally gave in to the dirty chaos. Michael and I didn't even have to clean our rooms with any regularity, which I guess was a bonus. But imagine what an animal smelling up the place would've done to our house. Shedded hair covering up our mess.

The two Alaskan Huskies across the street at the Jennings house, both of whom lived in red barn-shaped dog houses in a fenced-in pen outside, even in winter months, didn't exactly provide balance to deadly Cliff next door. Nor did they encourage me to love dogs any more than Cliff had. Jan and Claudia, names I never understood how they matched their violent Alaskan Husky personalities, barked nonstop. And with intent. It didn't matter whether it was 6 a.m., 3 p.m., or 10 p.m. Whenever they selfishly felt like it. I guess I'd be angry too if I came from freezing cold Alaska, but I still wouldn't threaten violence, at least not to a nice boy like me. Jan was the angrier of the two. She barked as if she and her sister were not fed blood-dripping, raw ribeye steaks soon, they would have no choice but to break out of their nine foot tall pen, jump over the six-foot wooden fence surrounding the Jennings' backyard and then rush to our house for an all you can eat ten-year-old boy buffet. I figured the only reason there was a giant fence was because Jan and Claudia were dangerous, ferocious beasts and needed to be contained. Then to have another six-foot fence if the first line of defense didn't work confirmed their obvious violent proclivities even more. Just my luck that Jan lived to be seventeen years old, well after I graduated high school.

In the fifth grade, I had to walk to school after someone stole my bike. We didn't exactly live in the best of neighborhoods, so I wasn't all that surprised that my bike disappeared after accidentally leaving it outside one night. I suspected it was Mitch, who lived just three doors down, but I didn't want to make any accusations since he was a bit of a bully anyway. While walking to school allowed me certain freedoms to take short cuts through various yards and climb fences I couldn't do on my dirt bike, it also exposed me to the "domesticated" animal kingdom like never before. I wasn't a block from my house when a large German Sheppard approached me. I started panicking, knowing my life was about to meet its ugly end. But then something bizarre happened. Instead of devouring me like a dog bone covered in peanut butter, my new German Sheppard friend started licking me. He sat and stared at me with his doggie smile, tail wagging back and forth in sheer delight. I reluctantly pet him, still cautiously scared he would chomp off my hand. Instead of eating me, he quickly rolled on his back, begging me to scratch and rub his inviting belly. I obliged. Could it be? A friendly dog? A dog that didn't want to harass me? A dog that wasn't pondering how I tasted? Maybe I had misjudged an entire species without really giving them a chance. Maybe I had been racist against dogs.

I checked my new furry friend's dog tag. His name was Jack. I laughed, which disarmed me even more. Without any urging from me, Jack decided to follow me to school, like an old friend. Smiling at me nonstop. I had walked ten minutes when it appeared that Jack finally had gone his separate way, without even a lick goodbye. I continued to walk, rethinking my all-out hatred of dogs. As I digested the question over the next five minutes of my walk to school, an angry brown Pit bull began barking at me from behind a fence. And I mean barking in an I-am-going-to-rip-your-limbs-off kind of barking. Despite having a cousin who once had her face bitten by one of these monsters, I wasn't overly concerned with the threat from the wild beast since a sturdy fence separated us. Apparently I misjudged that one. The Pit bull had increased his anger by the second and literally jumped the five-foot tall wooden fence, now in full throttle attack mode, running straight for my tiny four-foot frame. I was a goner. My five minutes of "dogs are nice after all" thoughts were instantly erased. All these years of dog fear were finally justified. I started to ball like a baby, but before I could surrender, Jack re-appeared out of nowhere and like my own personal guardian angel, chased the Pit bull away. I ran the rest of the way to school, never to see either dog again.

Soon after Jack saved my life, the Simerson's house caught on fire. Apparently, Mr. Simerson was doing some kind of work with a blow torch in his basement and caused an explosion. It took three fire trucks, an ambulance and a paramedic to put it out. I hadn't seen this much action on Rose Hill Road since the neighbors across the street left their garden hose on in their backyard before they left town, and it flooded three adjacent houses. Thankfully, Mr. and Mrs. Simerson made it out of their burning house just fine, but Cliff wasn't so lucky. He was stuck inside and two firemen ran into the burning house to save him. It only took a few minutes, but there he was being carried out by a fireman across his arms, clouds of smoke in the background. Cliff was limp but his lungs moved ever so slightly. He no longer looked so menacing and for a moment, I felt sorry for my scariest adversary. The paramedic hooked an oxygen tank up to Cliff to help him breath again. He laid there virtually still for over an hour, the belly of his body moving in and out slowly as he sucked in and breathed out air into the see-through mask made for humans. I stared in disbelief as the Doberman wasn't barking at us anymore, not even realizing that firemen were still on ladders fighting a dangerous fire with their large hoses. For the first time I realized that Cliff wasn't such a bad dog after all. He had feelings just like everyone else.

Cliff survived, and while the Simersons moved out of our neighborhood before the next backyard baseball season, I missed the adventures of watching Aaron retrieve baseballs in Cliff's quarters.

10

A Nice Jewish Boy in Jordan

"Tell me for the third time why an American Jew wants to visit Jordan?"

It was as this point I had pulled rank on the Israeli border security team carrying automatic weapons on their shoulders.

"I'm an American citizen with an American passport. I want to visit Jordan."

The Israeli security at the Aqaba-Eilat border crossing all but begged me not to cross into Jordan.

"It's not safe."

"You're risking your life."

"It's just stupid to not go on a tour as part of a group if you want to go there."

I was visiting my cousin Ella in Israel and we had decided to fly to the resort town of Eilat for a couple days of snorkeling and beach time. I had heard Eilat was beautiful.

"Look over there, Jeffrey. That's Jordan."

A day prior, Ella had pointed across the vast water to the Arab neighbor to the east. It made me curious. The only time I had met anyone from Jordan was in an airport heading to San Francisco and we hit it off splendidly. I had known Palestinians, Pakistanis, Egyptians, and others from the Middle East for many years. I already knew that Middle Eastern culture typically was warm and friendly. But I also knew that attitudes toward Israel and Jews in many of these countries was not so positive and in some cases downright anti-Semitic. Still, I couldn't bring myself to believe most people in any place are bad.

"It's so close," I responded to Ella. "How far is the closest border crossing?"

"Probably a ten-minute drive," she said with a reluctant tone.

"I want to visit. I want to see what it's like over there. To visit a real city in Jordan."

"No way!" she said in a defiant tone without any hesitation. "I absolutely am not crossing into Jordan unless it's to go on a tour to Petra or some other touristy spot."

"Oh, c'mon, Ella."

"No. No. No. Not going."

"Well, I'm going there tomorrow," I exclaimed back. "I will cross the border at 9 a.m. and be back for a late dinner."

"You're crazy, Jeffrey. You have to realize it's very dangerous. They don't like us. There are terrorists there, too."

I had tuned her out by this point, instead nervously dreaming of having my own personal peace mission. I hadn't even thought about crossing into Jordan when I planned my trip to Israel. My heart raced with excitement and some trepidation from how scared Ella was for me.

After forty minutes of arguing with Israeli border security, they had no choice but to let me cross. I approached the Jordanian guards on the other side of the border, observing the several pictures of King Abdullah hanging at the entrance. "Welcome to the Hashemite Kingdom of Jordan," read one large sign with the handsome king's picture beneath.

"What brings you to Jordan," a woman in covered hair kindly asked me at the first border crossing counter.

"Just want to meet people and shop."

The woman smiled, asked me to fill out some paperwork, reviewed my passport, and then sent me to the next window.

I proceeded with excitement.

"Passport and entry form, please" the man at the next window asked me.

"What's the purpose of your visit," he asked me after looking over my documentation.

"Just to see your country, maybe shop some," I told him with an eager look on my face.

"How long do you intend to visit?" the agent asked. "Just for the day," I told him.

He then stamped a piece of paper and handed me back my unstamped passport. "Enjoy your visit."

"Could you please stamp my passport?"

"Sorry, we don't do that."

I didn't understand why. Maybe it had to do with my coming from Israel. I was disappointed but no point in asking any further. I left the crossing and excitedly proceeded down the road to the nearest taxi stand. I was officially in Jordan! I couldn't believe it.

There was a line of taxis waiting, but only a handful of people were crossing into Jordan that day. I approached the person in charge of assigning taxis.

"Where are you headed," he asked me. I had only encountered three people so far, but each smiled at me.

"Not sure. I just want to be taken to the center of the nearest real city. No tourist spots."

"Mohammed!" he shouted to one of the taxi drivers standing next to his car, smoking a cigarette. He said a few more words in Arabic and I was motioned to get in the red cab.

"*Marhaba*," I said to the driver with a smile. I had tried to memorize a few Arabic terms the night prior and understood this was a nice greeting to say to someone when you first meet them. It literally means Master of God. He knew I was an English-speaking American, but he smiled, responded in kind and drove us off to start my Jordanian adventure.

We drove for thirty to forty minutes, and then he told me he would drop me in front of the main city hall and from there I could just walk other places. There wasn't much conversation in the car since Mohammed's English was scant at best. I had already exhausted the few Arabic words I knew, other than a few curse words Israelis borrow from Arabic.

When I got out of the cab, I was surrounded by an already bustling city with lunatic drivers flying around corners at absurd speeds, men walking in mostly red and white Arab headdresses, women with covered hair taking their children to school and other Arab men dressed in secular clothes, jeans, t-shirts and all.

I hadn't eaten breakfast yet, so I walked for just a few minutes until I saw a kabob restaurant that was already open for business at 9:25 a.m. The menus were in Arabic, but fortunately they had pictures. I ordered a cardamom coffee and some beef kabobs. The owner of the restaurant knew enough English to engage me for a few minutes.

"Where you from? America?"

"Yes, from Colorado."

"Well, welcome to Jordan. You let me know if I help you."

We chit-chatted about the city and which ways I should walk. I slammed down the delicious kabobs and coffee, and in thirty minutes, I was on my way.

My first stop was an indoor-outdoor open area where Arab men were smoking hookahs at ten in the morning. I'm not much of a tobacco guy, but as soon as I walked up, a man asked if I wanted to take a few hits. I obliged, as several others joined me. They wanted to know where I was from. What I was doing there. Did I know anyone in Jordan. One man, about fifty years old, was particularly intrigued. He had never left Jordan in his life, except to find a wife in Syria. We talked sports, kids, America, Jordan. But we didn't discuss politics, except to mutually poke fun at Trump. That seemed universal. After a half hour of friendly discussion had lapsed, my new friend, Zaid, asked if I wanted to join him for tea at his house a few blocks away. He seemed sincere, so I agreed.

We entered his apartment on the third floor of a building, first passing several men dressed in full-on Muslim garb, all of whom greeted us with smiles. Zaid's wife was home and she immediately welcomed me into their home as her husband explained in Arabic why they had a new guest. She smiled warmly after his soft words and immediately went to the kitchen to prepare mint tea and bring us some Arabic cookie pastries. Zaid's apartment was small but cozy. I sat on a soft couch draped with mosaic patterned material. There were family pictures across the room. A Jordanian military medal. And a picture of the previous king, King Hussein. There was no television. The apartment smelled like the spices of the Middle East. I felt at ease.

"Thank you so much for inviting me in your home. This is the first time I've been in anyone's house in Jordan."

"Well, you're always welcome in our home," he said with his genuine smile.

We talked for an hour, and when the time felt safe and right, I confessed something that seemed to change his world.

"You know, Zaid, we're cousins."

"What do you mean," he asked curiously.

"I'm Jewish. Our forefathers both came from Abraham. That makes us cousins."

He smiled bigger than I had ever seen before. "You're Jewish? I never met a Jew!" His eyes widened like a kid being introduced to a Disney character.

"Well, don't worry. I left my horns in America."

We both laughed, and from the look on his face, he may actually have heard that about Jews at some point in his life.

After his initial shock, he stood up from the chair across from me, slowly walked towards me and embraced me with a tight hug and then kissed me on the cheek. "I'm so very happy to meet you, cousin!"

From that point forward, his ear-to-ear smile didn't leave his face.

I stayed for another thirty or so minutes, just chatting about family, looking at pictures of his kids and answering his questions about Jews, which I was happy to do. I then wished him a good day, and headed back to the center of town.

For the next couple hours, I went in and out of local shops, buying chess sets, spices, coffee beans and the like. Met a dozen or more friendly Jordanian men along the way, all welcoming their American visitor with smiles.

One man in particular, tall, gray-bearded and in his seventies, struck up a conversation while I perused the various herbs and spices sold out of large canisters, the smells blending in unison with each other.

"Are you from America?"

"Is it that obvious?" We both laughed.

"Yes. I live in Colorado. I am a Jewish American." I know it may sound like an odd thing to blurt out, but I started feeling like I was on my own personal peace mission to break down barriers. Just like Zaid, my new Jordanian friend didn't flinch. He just smiled warmly as we continued our discussion. At no point did I ever feel like I was in any danger, despite my confession in a country without any Jews. My new friend, Omar, was genuinely excited to meet me.

"You know what?" he asked excitedly after about ten minutes of conversation. "I want you to come for dinner tonight. One of my wives makes amazing food."

"One of your wives," I asked him laughing.

"Yes, I have two wives."

I was laughing harder, but not in a judging way.

"Omar! That's one wife too many!!" I said in a joking voice. "I'm still trying to find just one! Not fair!"

We both laughed.

"I really wish I could come for dinner, but I have to get back to my cousin in Israel for dinner."

Omar was disappointed, but you could tell from our interaction, he was still glad we met.

After grabbing a few delicious Arabic pastries at a bakery on the way back to the center of town, I began looking for a cab to take me to the border.

As I approached Israeli security to reenter my ancestral homeland, I felt hopeful for this world. Hopeful for humanity. I just had a beautiful experience as a lone Jewish boy in Jordan. And it felt good.

"Why were you in Jordan," the woman in military gear asked me as I approached the metal detectors to enter Israel. I gave them the same schpiel as before, and another two officers questioned me for ten minutes about what I bought, who I met, whether someone gave me something, etcetera. I wasn't really offended. I knew Israel had to keep its borders safe.

The next morning Ella and I headed to the Eilat Airport to fly back to Tel Aviv. She passed through security in two minutes, but I wasn't so lucky. I still had the stamped paper showing I was in Jordan stuffed in the pages of my passport.

"Come with me!" an Israeli security guard motioned me to a separate room.

"Why were you in Jordan?" the muscular six-foot Middle Eastern man asked me in a thick Israeli accent.

"Just to visit," I said politely.

"Visit who," he demanded.

"Nobody in particular. I just wanted to meet people and shop."

"Who did you meet? What are their names? Did you accept any friend requests on Facebook?" he rattled off question after question, his voice raising more each time. Sometimes he didn't even wait for my response.

I continued answering him politely, trying to explain what I was doing there, but he wasn't buying it.

"No Jew just goes by himself to Jordan without something going on," as he continued expressing his rejection of my explanations.

Forty-five minutes of aggressive questioning and I finally had enough.

"I actually was visiting Israel on behalf of the Colorado Jewish Federation to teach elected officials in my state about how wonderful Israel is," I said in a purposely sarcastic tone.

"You can go through," he motioned me back into the airport lounge without further comment.

Maybe I'd been naïve about the dangers of the Middle East for a few moments. Maybe I wanted to be. I couldn't accept that most people in Jordan or anywhere else don't want what the rest of us want. Peace. Love. Friendship. Family. I get it. I'm not an Israeli who has to live next to lots of people who want it gone. But I never want to entirely get that. What I realized is that when you grow up in a sometimes rough neighborhood, you yourself can become rough and lose your humanity. I had enough blinders on to allow myself to enjoy Jordanians as they are. People.

Nice to meet you, Zaid and Omar.

11

Writer's Karma

"Take a look at these revisions and then come talk to me, Jeffrey."

I had just proudly turned in my first assignment as a lawyer the day before. August 2, 1995. I got an A in legal research and writing in law school, was always congratulated by professors on my writing in undergrad and, as a result, I knew I must have been a rockstar writer.

Before the redline feature on computers, people used to revise documents using a pen. This particular partner used a red pen, and I doubt it had anything to do with his favorite color. My "masterpiece" assignment he gave back to me had more of his red ink than the typed black print of my final work product. I was in shock. How could this be? I began reading through the comments. Setting aside the twelve typos he caught, he basically re-wrote the entire document.

"Here's the thing, Jeffrey," he started as we sat in one of his thousand-dollar fancy, burgundy leather chairs in his large corner office overlooking the skyline of St. Louis. "You waited

79

until page six to even tell the court what the document was about. You gave no roadmap of what you were arguing. Your writing was choppy. There was no story. Next time I want you spending as much time on the intro as the rest of the brief."

I could feel swarms of tears welling behind my eyes, but I kept my composure until I got back to my office. Maybe I wasn't cut out for this lawyer thing after all. Was I really *that* bad of a writer? It was 1995 and I hadn't even received the bar exam results back. Maybe I failed that too, I thought. Why would all my professors and teachers over the years praise my writing if it was so awful? I was left in a daze, but after the shock wore off, I remained determined to do it right next time.

Mr. Higgins wasn't the easiest lawyer to work with as it was, but underneath his black- and-white, Republican former prosecutor hard shell, he actually seemed to care about my future. Over the ensuing two years, he took the time to red-ink every one of my assignments, constantly giving me new tips and suggestions on how to improve my writing. I mean, he could have just revised the documents himself and had his secretary make the changes without even involving me. But every time he sat me in his fancy office with pictures of him with Ronald Reagan and George Bush on the wall staring down at me, he coached me how to improve my writing. I was especially fortunate because Mr. Higgins wasn't just a lawyer, he was a former writer for the *St. Louis Globe-Democrat*, one of the two major newspapers in St. Louis until it shut down in 1986. He had experience writing real stories.

Separate from law, I always wanted to be a writer. I was active in Israel, race, and other political issues in college, and thought I could one day be a syndicated columnist, like Maureen Dowd, Cal Thomas, or Thomas Friedman. So after a year of red ink from Mr. Higgins, I decided to write my first op-ed piece and submit it to the editorial board of the *St. Louis Post Dispatch* for publication. I told Mr. Higgins of my plan.

"Don't get your hopes up, Jeffrey. It's incredibly difficult to get an op-ed piece published. I highly doubt that's going to happen for you."

Not exactly what I wanted to hear, but I wasn't going to give up my dream of getting my op-eds published, no matter how much I respected him.

Only three days had passed when I picked up the morning paper and *voila!* My piece was published as the main writer on the guest columnist page. First try!

"Steve! Steve! You're not going to believe this! I got it published!!" It felt weird calling my decades-older mentor Mr. Higgins Steve, but everyone in the office used first names. "Let me see that," he demanded a copy of the paper, thinking maybe I was pulling his leg. "He looked over the paper for a good seven minutes before looking up at me, and just said, "Good work. Good work."

I didn't get much work done in the office the day the paper came out with my op-ed. I made scores of copies, sending them to friends everywhere. Email had just come out a year or two prior, so I was sending copies to the people I knew had them. I also began plotting my next writing move. I was going to start submitting op-eds to regional Jewish newspapers and other major newspapers.

Over the ensuing month, I went for the gold, submitting unsolicited pieces to *The New York Times, Washington Post,* and *Chicago Tribune.* Then I waited. I checked everyday. Nothing. Maybe my first piece was a fluke and Mr. Higgins was right. After all, I was only twenty-seven years old, just a year out of law school. Maybe I needed more Mr. Higgins red ink to take things to the next level. Still, I wasn't giving up.

I waited a few months and just continued racking up billable hours at the 300-person law firm. Billable hours were everything there, so I wasn't positioned to focus on extracurricular writing anyway. Finally, I mustered the courage to begin writing again and submitted another op-ed on the Middle East to the *St. Louis Post Dispatch*. Over the next few years, I submitted pieces published in the *Utah Star Tribune*, *The Ohio Jewish Chronicle*, *The Connecticut Jewish Ledger*, *The St. Louis Jewish Light,* and a few other smaller presses. I was getting published left and right. All said and done, I probably published two dozen pieces in a relatively short period of time. Then it happened.

"Mr. Kass. This is Mr. Rothstein. You are to come to my office immediately when you get here."

This was the message left on my voicemail on March 12, 1998. Mr. Rothstein was one of the top partners at my law firm. He was Jewish like me, but was known as a bully and someone you didn't want to mess with. Very intimidating. He was missing a finger on his left hand, but I never dared ask how that happened. Anyway, that's not the kind of voicemail you want from Mr. Rothstein. Heck, no kind of voicemail is one you wanted from him.

I didn't even bother to drop my raincoat and briefcase in my office. I took the elevator to the thirty-third floor where his office was located and walked in with the look of fear all over me.

"Good morning, Mr. Rothstein. You wanted to see me?"

"Close the door," he responded in an already nasty tone.

"You fuckin' listen to me, you little piece of shit pest. You're gonna stop writing. We have clients who don't like what you write."

I was confused. I never wrote about anything legal in nature nor did I write about any industries of clients we represented. Our firm represented tons of big casinos, but I never wrote an op-ed piece about the ills of gambling.

Mr. Rothstein continued after he realized how things came out. "Let me rephrase. I'm not telling you not to write, but I highly suggest for the security of your career you consider not writing anymore."

"Okay. I won't write anymore," I feebly responded as I left his office with my head down.

Mr. Rothstein wouldn't give me any details about who said what and when, but I knew it had nothing to do with clients. What I learned months later was that a few of the big wigs in the Jewish community were angry I'd been writing articles criticizing the Oslo peace accords signed by Israel. Ironically, my views have swayed much further to the left over the past twenty years, but then and now, I thought that type of censorship of ideas was wrong. It's not like my articles ever defamed any group or were derogatory in any way. When I left Rothstein's office, I was angrier than I was sad. Were my First Amendment free speech rights just violated? Could he threaten my career over this? Since my family had no money and I had no safety net, I couldn't afford to test out the theory. I never sent another op-ed piece to any major newspaper after that, and by 9/11 a few years later, I stopped writing political pieces altogether. In my mind, my writing career had come to an end.

Eventually, I switched to another large downtown law firm and settled in my career as a trial lawyer. One day, while driving home from the office at the typical seven o'clock evening hour, the news on the radio caught my attention.

"St. Louis lawyer and Democratic donor Michael Rothstein has pleaded guilty to two counts of fraud and one count of falsifying information to the Election Commission, admitting that he falsified bills to clients, illegally laundered money from other lawyers to give to politicians, and bested the system to help casinos get licenses to operate in Missouri." He had to forfeit his law license and resign from the prestigious law firm he once threatened me with termination.

I'm not typically a vindictive person, but I couldn't help think that this guy had it coming. He was known throughout the law firm as always treating people like shit. Demeaning and intimidating people. All of the younger associates were afraid of him. And rightfully so. But all his bullying and nastiness, his "I'm bulletproof" approach to life, had come crashing down.

Best of all, I got to write again.

12

They Call Me Nigger Lover

Until the sixth grade, I only knew one black kid. James. He was studious, smart, and other than the color of his skin, he was basically the same as the rest of our twenty-six white classmates, plus one Asian kid, at Olde Orchard Elementary. He spoke the same way. Lived in the same white neighborhood as most of the other classmates. He liked the same cartoon characters. He played on our little league baseball team, although he wasn't that coordinated so he mostly sat on the bench. None of us kids really thought much about his color. He was just James. Smart, straight-A student James. He later would go on to be valedictorian at our high school.

It was 1980 and the big talk in the Columbus public school system was desegregation. I didn't know what this meant at eleven years old, but I overheard my parents discussing how some judge a couple years ago ordered the schools to develop a program to integrate. They eventually called it bussing. Where black and white kids would have to take school busses to different school districts far away from their own neighborhoods. The goal was to make the schools a tossed salad of race. So when I showed up for sixth grade at Yorktown Middle School, I had new bussed-in classmates. Lots of them. James was no longer the only kid with darker skin. Half my class was, and they were nothing like James.

Some were smart. Some were dumb. Some spoke with some sort of slang effect I had only heard the few times I watched the sitcom *Sanford and Son*. Many of the new dark-skinned boys were good at sports. They didn't all like the same cartoons, though. Instead of going to video arcades each weekend, they largely preferred rollerskating rinks. Every Friday night at United Skates of America. I had never even been rollerskating. Most of the kids were from the inner-city neighborhood Olde Towne where Mom taught Fifth grade, near Ohio and Champion Avenues. Poor, mostly black and depressed areas. Boarded up homes. Occasional loud stereo systems blasting out of early model large American cars with broken mufflers. Oldsmobile Cutlass Supremes. Chevy Novas. Always a few people just walking around the streets smoking cigarettes. At least that's what I saw the few times Mom took me to her school to help make her bulletin boards before the year began.

The not so funny thing is our pothole-infested street wasn't much better. The four blocks of streets surrounding our house on Shenandoah Drive hadn't been repaved in at least two decades. But our neighbors were all white. Lower middle class laborers. An occasional semi-truck Peterbilt cab parked four doors down from our thirteen-hundred square foot one-car garage house. Cars on blocks, with neighbors sometimes underneath them doing repairs that never seemed to get finished. Lots of Republicans. We were shunned as the only family with a foreign-made vehicle, with our Japanese Datsun 210. Everyone else only bought American. After all, the Japanese bombed Pearl Harbor. Oh, and lots of American flags. Our neighbor Mr. Edwards actually had a twenty-five foot flag pole in his front yard like the kind you see at schools. We were the only Jews on our street. Heck, we were the only Jews I knew who lived in a neighborhood like ours. We also were the lone Democrats.

I wasn't afraid of our new classmates, unlike many of the other white kids. But I was definitely curious. Who were these dark-skinned kids? They were different and I wanted to know why.

"Hey, I'm Jeff. What's your name," I asked the five-foot nine sixth grader sitting next to me in homeroom the first day of school. Terrence's skin was way darker than James's. "Terrence, but my teammates call me Big T," he responded with a wide smile. Over the next six months of homeroom, Big T and I talked about everything eleven year olds talked about. Television. Sports. Girls. Our families. Music. More girls. But I watched *Superman* and *Wide World of Sports*. He watched *Fat Albert* and the Harlem Globetrotters. I had listened to the Eagles and The Cars. He was listening to Michael Jackson and New Edition. I enjoyed *Andy Griffith* and *Happy Days*, while he was busy laughing hysterically at *Good Times* and *The Jeffersons*. I played baseball. He played basketball. He knew how to dance. I could barely do the bunny hop. And on and on it went. I had no idea there was an alternate universe just a forced bus ride away. The other new kids I met, Leonard, Talia, Sharice, Theo, and Ben to name a few, pretty much liked the same things as Terrence. Sure, they all had their own unique flavors, but the black kids lived in a world I was only now discovering.

It wasn't just new music or different television shows, though. There was something about these kids that was fundamentally different. They had a deeper laugh. The way they hugged and greeted each other. How they smiled. The way they clasped hands in a you're-really-my-brother kind of way. The comfortable and relaxed way they spoke to each other. A camaraderie among them that I had never seen before. I knew they had something the rest of us didn't, and I wanted in on the secret. I devoured every morsel of education from my new friends and remained in awe of their world.

Things were sailing along just fine for my three years of middle school when a tall, lanky black kid named Derrick approached me at recess. Derrick transferred to our school for Eighth grade. He sat next to me in math class. The other kids around me quickly scattered away as Derrick walked closer toward me. I hadn't thought much of it, since my experience with the other black kids was fantastic. But Derrick had other plans for me.

"What's up, Jeff."

He knew my name even though we hadn't officially met.

"Hey, how are you," I responded, a growing feeling that something wasn't quite right festering in me.

"Here's the thing. You're going to help me pass math. On our test this Friday, I want you to sign language me the answers to each question." Derrick wasn't asking me to tutor him. He had asked me to cheat.

"I can help you learn, but I can't cheat on a test," I told him without hesitation. I hadn't ever entertained the thought of cheating in school. Well, except in Seventh grade typing class. I wasn't the best typist, so before Mrs. Armstrong started the timer for our tests, I would cough to cover up the sound of my slowly pressing a couple dozen keys to start typing the first two sentences of what we were about to be timed on. By the time the test started, I was already part way finished.

"Nah. That's not how it works here," Derrick firmly told me after I declined his cheating invite. "You're gonna sign language me the multiple choice answers. I'll teach you the letters A to E. If you don't help me, I'm gonna give you an ass-whooping next time I see you." Needless to say, that's how I learned to sign the letters A to E, and I still know them today. Not overly helpful for having conversations with deaf people. This was my first and last true bullying experience. Derrick had threatened to beat me up if I didn't help him. I didn't think I had much of a choice. "Just teach me the letters," I responded in a defeated voice.

The thing is, Derrick didn't scare me because he was black. He scared me because he was bigger than me and had threatened to kick my ass. I thought he was as different from the other scores of black kids I met, sort of like how James was different. Honestly, it probably just reinforced that any one of us is capable of good or bad and skin color isn't the deciding factor. It didn't dawn on me at the time that Derrick had bullied other white kids, too.

High school wasn't much different than middle school, except now I was attending school with a hundred and thirty black kids in my almost three-hundred kid freshman class. They were everywhere and I loved it. I gave up all connection to Aerosmith, Quiet Riot, and Van Halen in favor of Prince, Bobby Brown, and Johnny Gill. I passed on watching *The Dukes of Hazzard* and instead watched *Soul Train*. I began going to rap concerts. Run-DMC. The Fat Boys. Whodini. I even learned how to break dance a ltitle.

American black culture spoke to me. As a teenager it wasn't about racial justice or pretending to be someone I wasn't. I was just enjoying myself. Even attending a black Baptist church for friends' events was an exhilarating experience. The singing, shouting, and dancing was nothing I ever saw in our synagogue and certainly nothing they did at my white Christian friend Billy's Protestant church for his childhood Passion of the Christ plays I had to attend. Oh the joys of watching us Jews kill Christ while Billy played one of the disciples. Those experiences were still bland and boring compared to a black church. I even briefly dated a black girl my junior year, although that didn't sit too well with my Democratic party white parents. "Jeff, mixed kids have so many problems," was Mom's lame excuse to try to talk me out of it. Honestly, I just wanted to kiss Tracy Taylor. Who the hell was thinking about kids?

When I graduated high school, I still wasn't truly aware of any major race issues. Sure, we studied Martin Luther King, Jr. and slavery and even heard about the awful Apartheid regime in South Africa, but there wasn't a lot of talk about racism in my high school. I knew the Klan and other wacko hate groups still existed, but racism in everyday life never crossed my mind. I thought that stuff, like anti-Semitism, was mostly a thing of the past. You know, the 1960s. So when my friend Larry and I took Black Studies 101 our freshman year of college to fill our humanities requirement, I was in for a rude awakening. Not as much as the swastika painted on my dorm room door three months into college, but an awakening nonetheless.

Did you know that the traffic light was invented by a black man? The refrigerator. The carbon filament that goes inside Edison's light bulb to make it stay on. Peanut butter. I mean, c'mon. Peanut butter?! It doesn't get better than that. We ate Peter Pan as a kid, but now I prefer the Whole Foods no-sugar variety. The more I learned about black history, the more I started wondering why I never heard any of this in grade school. Or why my high school world history course taught us a lot about England, France, China and the like but suspiciously left out most of Africa, the birthplace of the library. It never crossed my mind that all of our images in society, black cats, black this and black that, were typically the dark, evil side, while white was always considered pure. No doubt these images had unknowingly crept into our collective psyche.

The proof was in the pudding. Classmate after classmate shared the horrors of their daily life experiences. Calling up apartment complexes in college to see if any units were available, but when they showed to see the supposedly available apartments, they were all of a sudden taken. Getting pulled over for speeding only to be asked to step out of the vehicle. That shit never happened to me. One guy, Freddie, got punched by a campus cop when he asked them why they were bothering him. Apparently cops got a call about a black man breaking into a store and Freddie was in the vicinity and matched the description. Black and male I'm guessing. The only thing good about that is Ohio State settled a lawsuit with Freddie for injuries he sustained in the sad incident and the rest of his college was paid for. The sad stories never seemed to end.

The black studies course wasn't just a good education. It made me angry. Ignorance really was bliss, but now that I knew what was taking place in society, now that I knew what my fellow black friends experienced on a daily basis, I wanted justice. Dad had pounded into my head for years that we wouldn't tolerate anti-Semitism. Ironic that this was the same dad who voted for Trump. Why would I tolerate similar bullshit directed toward my black friends? "Fuck all the haters" was my new mantra. I was out for blood. For the rest of college and law school, I was on a mission to pounce on anyone and everyone who was racist or anti-Semitic.

I took a political science course about Latin America during my sophomore year. Bernard, who I met at a black fraternity party the previous year, was in my class. He was the studious type. A member of the black fraternity Phi Beta Sigma, which was known to have smarter, nicer, and sometimes nerdier kids. Bernard fit the Sigmas' stereotype. He was six-foot four, a little on the heavier side, and wore black, horn rim Malxom X glasses. He was a 4.0 student, attending Ohio State on a full academic scholarship. So of course, I wanted to study with him.

"Meet me at my fraternity house at 8 p.m.," I told Bernard after class one day. "We'll quiz each other for the test this Friday." Midterms were upon us and I always did well on tests using flash cards. A bit elementary school-ish of me, but it worked. Any time I used flash cards or some similar quizzing method, I got an A. Bernard showed up on time, knocking on the glass back door of my Jewish fraternity house. Five of my so-called brothers were sitting in the main room twenty feet from the door, when Bernard stood waiting after he knocked a few times.

Johnny looked up. "Holy shit. Let's get the fuck out of here." Like sheep, the other four white college students ran out of the room. Scared stiff that a large black man had come to our house. I was president of the fraternity at the time, so they ran to my room. "Jeff, I think we need to call the cops. There's a huge black dude at our back door." I wasn't ever the type to be scared of people. I calmly walked out and saw Bernard standing outside in the twenty-degree Ohio snowy winter evening. I opened the door and Bernard already figured out what had gone down. "Those motherfuckers," was all he said in the first livid tone I had heard out of his mouth since meeting him. Bernard wasn't the type to anger easily. A calm, usually smiling man. A soft, warm voice. But even good people have their limits.

All I could muster at the time was "Brother, I'm so sorry. Unfortunately, Jews aren't immune from the same racist attitudes of the rest of society." I always wanted to think that Jews were *less racist* than other white folks, even evolved dare I say. To some extent that really is the case, but let's face it, Jews are part of the same system we all are. They went to the same high schools. Had the same images. Saw the same white superheroes. Yes, Jews are typically involved in fighting bias more than their non-Jewish white peers, and many of the kids lynched and jailed in the South fighting bigotry were Jews, but at the end of the day, Jews in America are still white, still enjoy the benefits of being the dominant skin color, and often don't get it. This became particularly true as many Jews moved up the economic ladder. To Bernard's credit, we still studied, still got As, and he didn't personally blame me for that awful night in February. Bernard never let the mud of society get in his way.

Racist fraternity incident aside, I wasn't expecting one of my fraternity brother's non-Jewish friends, Doug, to verbally attack me after Bernard left. *Nigger lover*, Doug whispered in my ear with a laugh and wide ear-to-ear smile. Doug was a good six inches taller than me, had arms the size of my thighs, and a shaved head. Almost like a Nazi skinhead, but I think he just played lacrosse for Ohio State's club team and all of his teammates had shaved heads. Actually, I never even noticed the skinhead resemblance until the n-word comment. I just looked at him with a "I feel sorry for you" kind of stare. Not sure this was a teaching moment for guys like him.

Doug wouldn't be the first one to call me that name in one form or another over the ensuing twenty years. My girlfriend after my divorce yelled it at me during an argument after

I forgot to pick her up from work earlier that day. Nothing to do with race. Officially, her version was *you fuckin' nigger lover.* Friends of friends have faux-jokingly referred to me as that for years, although I never got the humor in it. Most of the time, well-meaning friends or girlfriends only curiously asked, "Why do you like black people so much?" Funny, though, they never asked me why I like white people, or Jewish people, or any other group of people. Somehow having too many close black friends needs an explanation white people can understand.

Even after seven years of college and law school, hearing and witnessing all kinds of racist crap, when I graduated and began working for a major law firm, I figured racism would subside. At least in the professional world I was about to enter. I should've known better. I wasn't a month into my new job when I found myself in a partner's office in the Mercantile building in downtown St. Louis with a former U.S. Democratic senator and two wealthy Democratic Party donors all talking about how to improve the city. The partner, Michael, was animated about fixing the downtown area. Michael was a wealthy real estate lawyer and had all kinds of ideas how to develop the many dilapidated streets that plagued St. Louis's core. I don't remember how I even ended up in the meeting, but I felt so privileged as a brand new twenty-six-year-old lawyer to be in a room with all of these movers and shakers. And to think they were all self-proclaimed left wing liberals made it that much better since I typically agreed with the left's general philosophy of helping the most disadvantaged.

"Bottom line, though, is we aren't fixing a goddamn thing in this city if we don't get rid of all the black people downtown."

What? Did I really just hear a wealthy, liberal *Democrat* lawyer tell an also liberal former U.S. senator that black people needed to be cleared out? I wanted to speak up. But then I remembered how badly I needed my job, seeing that my parents had nothing and if I was going to make it in this world, I needed to earn a living. Sadly, this type of attitude was repeated in my professional circles for years. Didn't matter whether it was coming from left or right wingers.

These unfortunate experiences only caused me to double and triple my personal efforts. I became involved in multiple civil rights and empowerment organizations. I volunteered in inner-city schools. I tutored kids. While I never fixed the world through these efforts, which always seemed to come up short, I did befriend dozens and dozens of great men and women in the black community over the years. Just like high school and college, I was welcomed as a family member. Invited into their churches, barbecues, family gatherings, and parties. Kids of friends call me Uncle Jeff. Some friends started calling me White Chocolate. One friend, Rick, calls me Cream, telling me I was a mix of black and white. When my 23andMe and Ancestry DNA tests came back two percent north African (to be fair, Algerian and Moroccan), I couldn't wait to tell friends I was no longer White Chocolate. Now I should be called Two Percent. Not regular milk. Two Percent.

While society has gone through many changes since middle school, what didn't change was the brotherly, familial, and loving atmosphere that pervades life in black America. The time I spend at black family gatherings, in organizations, at parties, or even a night out remains the deepest part of my life. It's not lost on me the irony of a society that portrays black folks as hard, mean, and angry, when in reality, the rest of us could learn quite a bit in how we treat each other. We could all learn to hug more. To clasp hands like we care about each other. To create bonds that go beyond small talk and nice pleasantries.

The black community has its own severe issues, no doubt, but love isn't one of them.

The next time a white friend asks me why I love black people, which I am sure will be any day now, I plan on responding *brotherhood*.

13

Fuck You, Sugar!

For forty-nine years old, I thought I looked pretty good. I worked out three days a week for a year, and people regularly told me I looked more like thirty-seven. My three teenage kids thought I looked and acted super young. While I loved a good ice cream cone or pizza from time to time, and I certainly loved funky restaurants, I ate way healthier than most people I knew. Even made peanut butter spinach smoothies from time to time.

Then I met Rebecca. She was a fitness trainer and it showed. She was the epitome of in-shape. Arms, legs, butt. Fit as fit can be. Only previously dated iron man kinda guys. Buff. Hundred-mile bike ride type freaks of men. Twelve-day treks through the Amazon kind of psycho guys.

"I'm not sure we're compatible," she told me on our first date. "I don't typically date guys as out of shape as you. You have a belly."

I couldn't believe a complete stranger had just blatantly insulted me. I didn't think I had a belly, and I never had problems getting dates with attractive women. Plus, I felt like my muscles had grown significantly in the past year since I had been going to a personal trainer at a kettlebell studio three days a week. I was generally happy with my appearance. And what kind of values did this woman have anyway, focusing on that instead of whether I was kind or intelligent or a good person?

"Did you just body shame me?" I reacted. "Imagine if a man had said that to a woman on a date. A first date even. You're right, we're not a good match." I shook my head in disgust. That was the end of that. Who does that kind of thing?

"Wait! I'm not saying we can't date," she reacted. "But it's not shallow for wanting to date a person who takes care of themselves. I'm sure you don't want to date a woman who is overweight, do you?"

I guess she had a point in that we all have certain physical preferences, but I still felt so angry and ashamed. Why did she need to express them rather than just say "nice to meet you" and move on. Despite my anger, I thought long and hard about some things she'd said to me. "After one year of training three days a week, you should be ripped by now. Who the hell is training you? Do you do any cardio? And your diet is awful. You eat way too many carbs and sugar."

As unkind as her methods were, she did have a point. Why wasn't I a thousand times more in shape? Why hadn't I lost even a few pounds after a year? In fact, I had gained ten pounds, with my previous trainer telling me it was all muscle gain. I even had clothes tailored to make them fit my larger body. Alas, I wasn't the rockstar I thought I was. So I did something I've never done before when it came to my health. I took swift and immediate action to remedy the situation. I read a book about sugar and how addictive and destructive it is. I changed trainers to someone who was willing to push me harder. I added cardio a couple days a week. I started going on long, fast walks at night. And most importantly, I eradicated sugar and most unhealthy carbs from my diet. I switched to a mostly fish, chicken, nuts, and green veggies with healthier fruits type of diet. I did everything Rebecca mentioned. And with gusto and determination. I literally went a hundred days with no added sugar in any of its many forms and names.

Fast forward eight months. While I didn't end up marrying Rebecca, I dropped thirty-three pounds. I weigh the same thing I weighed my junior year of high school. My arms and abs are showing like never before. I no longer have to take Tums four to five times a day. Or itch every night. I feel the best I've ever felt in my entire life. I lost my craving for sweets and junk. And I'm just getting started. So thank you Rebecca, but fuck you, sugar!

14

Selfish Little Things

I wasn't a big fan, but Kim loved cats. I always thought they were rather useless and downright selfish creatures, but I still thought it would be nice to get her a kitten for her twenty-first birthday. We were both students at Ohio State and had been dating for over a year. I had never even heard of "rescues" in 1990, so I went to the pet store at the mall and bought a gray and white striped tiger looking cat. I think they called it a Tabby cat. Later that night, I surprised Kim.

"What's in the brown box," she asked smiling.

The kitten was making noises as if he was trying to escape, so I didn't hesitate any longer. It wasn't much of a surprise with all that commotion.

"Oh my god! It's so cute!!" Kim was so excited. "What should we name him?"

I loved fashion, so I suggested "Polo." Kim agreed.

I had already bought all the supplies to go with Polo. Litter, litter box, catnip toys (which I heard was like cocaine for cats), and the like. We played with Polo in my room at my fraternity house and then headed back to her sorority, Kappa Delta, to introduce Polo to his new home.

"Excuse me! What is that you have there?" Jane asked in a scolding teacher sorta tone, even though she was the same age as Kim. Jane was also a student at Ohio State and had been elected by Kim's sorority sisters as "house manager" to oversee all of the girls living in the Kappa Delta sorority house where Kim lived.

"It's my new kitty, Polo," Kim bragged. Kim hadn't picked up on the "oh-shit-you're-in trouble" words I knew were coming.

"Well, I'm sorry, but it's against Kappa Delta house rules to keep any animal here. Section 12.3 of the sorority code of conduct. He can't stay."

I didn't want there to be a scene, so I quickly interjected. "No problem. He can stay with me." I knew my disgusting fraternity house, the subject of multiple health code violations, wasn't going to object to one more smell.

I couldn't believe it, but I was now going to be the care-taker of a stupid cat. I definitely hadn't thought this through.

On night two of my new disaster, I woke up to the most nauseating smell. Three in the morning. Did the litter box need to be cleaned already? I walked into my bathroom to check. The smell wasn't coming from there. I looked everywhere but I couldn't pinpoint it. It was like a combination of cat piss, poop, and vomit. I opened all six of the windows in my room.

When I returned later that day, windows open for six hours, the smell had all but disappeared. Whew.

Night three.

When I woke up at four thirty in the morning to go to the bathroom, I again was greeted by the same disgusting smell. But after searching and searching, I still couldn't find the source. It was thirty-two degrees outside, but I had no choice but to open the windows again. I would have rather froze than vomit.

The smell debacle continued for weeks. While Kim thought it was pretty funny, I wasn't amused. I was ready to get rid of my new intruder. The problem was that Polo was actually pretty damn cute. He purred incessantly when I walked into the room. He followed me everywhere. I even taught him how to fetch blue Bic pens. I could throw one of those pens into another room and Polo would chase it down, put it in his mouth like a dog with a stick, and return it to me in seconds. Polo even came running when I called his name. He was basically a dog in a cat's body. That made it a bit hard to kick him out. Polo was my pal, no matter how bad he smelled or how much I tried to hate him.

Our friendship was really solidified when one of the resident drug abusers in our fraternity, Johnny, came knocking on my door to complain about something. I was the president of the frat, so I had to deal with whatever problems fifty guys all living under one roof might have. I didn't care much for Johnny. He was always rude to me, and there was tension between us since he knew I didn't approve of all his drug using. Polo, who had never so much as done anything but meow and purr, sprung out of nowhere as Johnny complained to me. Polo jumped on Johnny and put his claws right into his chest.

"Owwwww! What the fuck!!!"

I pulled Polo off Johnny as he left my room.

I don't know how he knew, but Polo obviously sensed Johnny's dislike for me, or mine for him.

While I didn't want anyone getting hurt, I'm not gonna lie. It was pretty funny. "Good boy, Polo," I told him in an approving tone. Johnny never bothered me in my room again.

I moved into an apartment the next fall, and when I removed my waterbed from the room, I finally discovered the origin of the smell. Scores of dried cat poop all along the back baseboard of the bed. Apparently, Polo had been sick and decided to just shit in the one place I couldn't see. Fortunately, petrified cat shit only smells for a couple months so I didn't have to endure it the entire year.

Kim and I broke up around the time of my move and, well, Polo was kind of my friend. Kim just played with him when she stayed over. Naturally, I would get Polo in the breakup. We didn't have any other shared assets! Plus, as much as Kim protested that decision, she really couldn't do anything about it living with the cat-free Kappas.

I was excited for Polo. Instead of being confined to one room, my new apartment had two bedrooms (I was rooming with my friend Scott), a living room, and a kitchen. Polo had lots more places to jump and play. This was my final year of college, but my first time living in an apartment. Before then, it was the dorms, and then the frat house.

College was pretty busy. I was working three jobs, taking classes, applying to law schools. I was finally involved in activities outside of my fraternity. And of course, I was going out several nights a week. My friend Alex and I would head to a reggae bar off campus at least three nights a week.

All that sounds great, except Polo had nobody to play with—that was until I got home from my seventeen hours of daily activities. Polo got all of his cat sleeping in during that time, so when I got home, he was wired and ready to roll. Kind of reminds me of the call centers in India. People who get off work at four or five in the morning their time to listen to us Americans complain all day. I hear they have bars and restaurants in India to cater to them when they get off work. An entire community partying at off hours.

At first it was cute. Polo would climb all over me in bed, licking me, purring, bringing me pens to throw. I didn't get much sleep the first couple nights, so I had no choice but to close my door and let Polo play in the rest of the apartment. That didn't work out so well. Polo wasn't interested in playing in general. He missed me and wanted my attention. I felt so bad for my furry friend, but I needed my measly six hours of sleep. Polo quickly figured out how to still get my attention. He learned to knock on the door with his paws, while I had to listen to the door move back and forth. I put a towel underneath the door to keep it from moving. Polo then cried and meowed so loud, it was worse than the door shaking. I tried putting things in front of the door, but Polo would just knock them down and cause even more noise. I put Polo in the bathroom, where his litter box was housed, but Polo just kicked around the shampoo, soap and other items laying around. After I put all that away, he starting wailing in a way I had never heard. This no-sleep routine went on for a month until I became a walking zombie. I couldn't take it anymore. I couldn't keep up with work, classes, and going out. I had to do something fast. I put signs up around campus, asking if anyone wanted to adopt an awesome cat. Three days more of no sleep and not one phone call.

At wits end, I called the closest pound. I asked a lot of questions.

"Will he be adopted?" I asked.

"Sorry, sir, we cannot guarantee that will happen. Some animals do, some don't."

"Well, do the really cute ones get adopted more often?" I pried further.

"Sir, we cannot comment on if, when, or how fast any animal will be adopted."

Not the answers I wanted, but I was out of options. I drove Polo to the pound, crying in the car. Polo always sat quietly in the front seat when we went for car rides together. He just looked at me with his adorable face, completely unaware this was going to be our last encounter.

"Well, Polo, be a good boy and I'm sure a nice family will adopt you soon," I said my goodbye, as I left him with the nineteen-year-old college student at the front desk.

"Are they going to kill him? How long do you guys wait? How long will you give it to see if he is adopted?" I wanted to know Polo was going to be okay, but the answers were the same as before. "We can't tell you that kind of information."

As I drove home, I had this urge to turn my car around and get Polo back, but I knew I couldn't continue the pattern of no sleep.

I tried calling again the next day. "Any chance you can tell me if that gray and white tiger cat was adopted yet? His name is Polo."

"Sorry sir, we can't give out that kind of information."

"Did you guys put him down?" I begged to know. My guilt was taking over me.

"Sir, we can't provide you any information about the cat."

For my own sanity, I had no choice but to imagine that Polo was adopted by a kind person who loved him and treated him like the adorable cat he was. That's how I still think of it today, twenty-eight years later.

15

Where Everyone Knows Your Name

The same two men, one blonde, about forty and always smiling, and the other about sixty with a long, well-groomed gray beard and noticeable blue eyes, meet for coffee here each weekday at the same time. 7:30 a.m. If it's not raining or snowing, they typically sit in the patio area in front where a fifty-year-old locust tree provides shade. On occasion they share a small table along the quieter wall at the rear of the shop. They started recognizing me a few weeks ago, pointing their genuine friendly smiles my way most mornings, although I don't keep as rigid a schedule as they do. The younger of the two is Adam. The bearded, always smiling man, Ken. After exchanging good mornings and hellos a dozen or so times, they finally decided to introduce themselves. I could have initiated myself as I've done with many others in the past, but I never wanted to interrupt their daily meetings. The conversations seemed important from the focused looks on their faces and raised eyebrows.

"Nice to meet you, Adam. Ken. I'm Jeffrey. So what is it you guys do that brings you here to Aviano each morning?"

"We're in development and construction. Working on a lot of those buildings you see going up around Cherry Creek."

Cherry Creek is a posh area of Denver with lots of shops, art galleries, and dining. But lately condos, office buildings, mixed use, and other new buildings have been springing up faster than dandelions. I guess some of it's good for Denver, but orange barrels and tall, mountain-view blocking cranes have become the norm here. You can't really turn a corner without running into a closed street, temporary fence, or men waving cars in different directions. Once in a while, I bring coffee to a few of the hardhat-wearing workers at the site near Aviano. Recently, I even asked a group of three of them to join me for coffee and pastries. They graciously accepted. A good way to start the day.

I tried my first cup of coffee in 1998 and it was gross. Granted, it was pre-ground grocery store bought instant Folger's French vanilla, but at the time I just knew coffee wasn't for me. Who needs an energy boost to start the day? I had that naturally. I actually didn't drink a single cup to get through college or law school. Mom drank decaffeinated black coffee at the Stump's grocery store café down the street when I was a kid and it never appealed to me. Never understood the point. I tried Starbucks years later when I was falling asleep driving two hours home for winter break and it wasn't much better. I'm not sure what caused me to give it another try a few years ago, but when I did, I fell in love. Aviano is a high-end coffee shop where they serve only the best sourced and roasted beans from the internationally known Intelligentsia brand. Rwanda, El Salvador, Ethiopia, Kenya, Bolivia. You name the exotic place, and they've served their coffee.

I typically order a pour over, where it takes Aviano manager James or man-bun teenage heart throb Patrick a good eight minutes to make my cup of joe. They grind the beans to just the right amount of fineness, then pour hot water over them until the coffee drips through a filter into a large glass beaker that looks like something out of a seventh grade science experiment. Then, *voila!* The best twelve ounces of coffee $5.40 can buy. That's right. Over five bucks for my morning coffee. Let's see. Five times six equals $30 a week. Except sometimes I come back for an afternoon one, too. Let's say five times nine. That's $45 a week, fifty-two times a year. Almost $2,400! Yikes.

Last month as I was sipping away on a nice Honduran blend, I began observing one of the regulars. A Hispanic looking six-foot-tall thin man covered in tattoos. Both arms. Neck. I'm sure other places too, although I didn't ask. I saw him there most mornings for several weeks. Very eclectic. Handsome. Usually wearing tight skinny jeans and assorted colored high tops. Always working away on his computer or on some conference call with his headphones. What important stuff was he up to? I started wondering.

"Hey my man. I've seen you here a ton. Thought I'd finally say hello," I approached him with some attempt at a cool guy tone to match his tattoos. He definitely was hipper than me, so I needed to at least seem cool.

"I'm David. Nice to meet you."

"So what is it you do?" I finally was going to get an answer to my curiosity.

"I'm a poet."

A poet? Now that wasn't in the world of possibilities swirling in my head. Who the hell meets a real life, published poet? Maybe some other kind of artist, like a musician or painter, but a poet?

We chatted a little longer. Talked about our families. I told him about my own writing.

When I got to the office, I had no choice but to look him up. He wasn't kidding. An award winning poet with his very own book, *Post Traumatic Hood Disorder.* Known coast to coast. I promptly ordered a copy. Not gonna lie. David Tomas Martinez is some of the best poetry I've ever read—and I accidentally happened to meet this great artist in my local coffee shop.

I don't typically read online reviews of restaurants or most food-related businesses. For some reason, bored in my son's orthodontist's office waiting room, I started perusing reviews of various places online, including Aviano. "Pretentious!" was the first one. "Uppity. People there think they're better than other people." There were some good ones, too, but the lot of reviews were peppered with these occasional swipes at the coffee shop just two blocks from some of the wealthiest neighborhoods of Denver. Aviano definitely has a certain flare of fanciness, but the people who work there are anything but stuck up. Students paying for college. Immigrants just trying to make ends meet in their new country. Graphic artists who need a little extra money. Twenty somethings trying to figure out what they want to do in life. It's not exactly like the employees pouring the coffee somehow have chips on their shoulders. A few minutes of conversation with any of them would reveal the opposite. Genuine. Real. Caring. Even deep. One guy who used to work there, Zach, is one of the most sincere and sensitive people I've ever met.

The patrons aren't all high rollers either. Okay, some of them are, but most aren't. Charlie arrives promptly at 8 a.m. each day with a book to read. He worked for twenty-five years in state government and recently was laid off. Trying to figure out his next career move, at age fifty-eight. Charlie is short at five-foot six, thin, with a three-day stubbled gray beard and wire-rimmed glasses. Soft spoken and gentle. He graciously bowed his head in thanks one morning when I took care of his coffee bill.

Everyday by mid-afternoon Aviano fills up with dozens of Arabs from various Persian Gulf countries. Kuwait, Saudi Arabia, UAE, and others. I'm guessing they all refer to it as the Arabian, not Persian, Gulf because of hostilities with Iran. These patrons are all super wealthy, well dressed, and always speak in Arabic. Mostly handsome, distinct looking men, but occasionally a few women wearing headscarves. Even an occasional twenty something young man in a white robe with a red and white ghutrah. A Ferrari sometimes parked outside still has a license plate from Qatar. They mostly keep to themselves, although for months I've been trying to strike up a conversation. *Marhaba,* I sometimes say to greet a few of them. It literally means "God is love" but is used as a friendly greeting among Arabs. I get an occasional smile back, but mostly just nods of the head. I'm sure they are apprehensive about how they are viewed in the U.S., so some white guy greeting them in Arabic might not always be welcome. Once I got lucky. I was sitting outside on the patio. Aviano was packed, so patrons were sitting in closer quarters to each other. I decided to give conversation with my Muslim cousins another shot.

"How's your day," I decided to start in English.

"Great, how about yours," the thin, twenty-two or twenty-three-year-old kid responded with a genuine smile.

After we exchanged a few more pieces of small talk, we spoke about where each of us was from. Ohio and Qatar. Corn and Hummus. Not exactly an even exotic match. When my new friend Saif asked about my real background, I divulged that I am Jewish. For some reason, I never was afraid to reveal my Jewish identity. I always viewed it as an opportunity to make up for negative media portrayals or bad experiences. Or to correct a wrong perpetrated by one of my co-religionists.

Saif perked up when I said the word "Jewish," and that's when the conversation got interesting. He was visibly intrigued. He had never met a Jew but didn't have the negative views I assumed he was taught growing up in a country totally devoid of them. I had imagined images of Israeli soldiers shooting tear gas into a scattering Palestinian crowd as his television reference point. We talked for a good hour, not at all following the social protocol of avoiding religion and politics. Judaism and Islam are quite similar in their structure, have similar laws, and even share many of the same prophets. When Saif learned that Jews don't eat pork, bury their dead immediately, and have an entire system of legal debates and opinions that determine Jewish law, he couldn't believe it, as Islam shares all of those things. Makes you wonder why those two religions have been at odds for so long. We said our goodbyes, shook hands with a smile, and looked forward to running into each other again soon at Aviano. "So nice to meet you, my cousin," Saif said to me as we parted ways. I smiled back.

The biggest problem with Aviano isn't whether the coffee costs too much or whether its placement in a rich neighborhood makes it too pretentious. Honestly, it's that I'm drinking too much coffee now.

16

The Privilege Is All Mine

The latest call by a white woman to 911 over what turns out was just a black man entering his own apartment in St. Louis brought out the white privilege discussion again.

The thing is, words matter.

Author and activist Dr. Nita Mosby Tyler recently was discussing the word "diversity." We equality activists have used that word for decades now to mean black. Or Jewish. Or Hispanic. Women. Gay. But it got lost on us that diversity does not mean only those groups. It means all of us. A diverse classroom includes black, brown, gay, Jewish, and yes, white. A diverse workforce likewise includes white folks along with all those other groups. When we say we want a diverse set of opinions and experiences at the table, that by definition should include everyone. Not just minorities. We made a colossal mistake, according to Dr. Mosby Tyler, by equating diversity with just minorities. It may have not been intentional, but we all know when we hear the word diversity, it now only means minority. We left people out of the discussion.

The phrase "white privilege" seems to fall into that same trap. I drive to work, get pulled over for speeding, and the cop writes me a ticket while I sit in my heated-seat vehicle, ass nice and warm. Nobody ever asks me to step out of my car. I call up an apartment complex to inquire if there are available units, and lo and behold when I show up forty-five minutes later, an available apartment is still there. They didn't abruptly run out of the four units I was told on the phone I could see. The way it's supposed to be. And so life goes on without incident. Stew on that for a second. Is it a privilege to be treated as a normal human being? Most white folks would never think of it that way, because isn't that how life is supposed to work?

When George W. Bush was President, Chris Rock had this to say about white privilege: "A black C student can't even be the manager at Burger King. Meanwhile a white C student just happens to be the President of the United States of America!"

Forget George Bush. Can you imagine if Obama had multiple ex-wives, kids from different women, screwed porn stars, paid someone to have an abortion, and was rumored to be involved in golden showers from Russian women? Trust me, we wouldn't be discussing approval ratings wavering between 34 and 40 percent. Even white Dems would've jumped ship long before then.

Still, what the phrase white privilege does is put white folks on the defense for just living life as a normal human being should. To enter their own damn apartment without being suspected of a crime. Indeed, at no point have I ever pondered how privileged I was to enter my own place of abode without being suspected of criminal activity. Why would I?

I attend Denver Nuggets basketball games quite frequently. As you can imagine, there are unruly or obnoxious fans at many games. I'm a Buckeye myself, and we can be pretty ridiculous with our devotion to Ohio State sports teams. I've definitely dropped a few f-bombs watching my Buckeyes botch a play or lose a game they shouldn't have. When we lost to Michigan State a few years ago, I screamed more curse words in one quarter of football than the entire year. I'm not proud of my dive into the abyss of classlessness. The level of obnoxious at sporting events really knows no race, age, or gender boundaries. White professionals screaming at refs. Rednecks yelling expletives at other fans. Black folks screaming "you suck" to players on the other team. It really is all the same in one form or another. I mean, c'mon, we have to support our teams, right? So at a Nuggets game last year, sitting next to a morbidly obese black man dropping "Fuck you, piece of shit Nuggets!" and "Pussies!" here and there, my then girlfriend whispered in my ear, "This is what gives black people a bad name." I gave her a puzzled look but quickly responded. "I've seen quite a few people of all shapes and sizes say the same shit at sporting events for many years." Don't get me wrong. The yelling was way over the top, but why is it whites don't get group-blamed when some lone, disturbed white man shoots up an entire place? And then the shooter is immediately called mentally disturbed or partially excused for having some psychological disability.

In 1996, fresh out of law school, my friend Reggie, who is also a lawyer, stopped by the diamond counter at Famous Barr (now Macy's) in downtown St. Louis. He returned to work angry and flustered. Reggie was dressed in a gray pinstriped suit and was there to pick out an engagement ring for his girlfriend. Our law firm Thompson & Mitchell was quite conservative, and back then it required all the lawyers to wear suits everyday.

The woman at the jewelry counter told Reggie he could only look at one diamond at a time. And that he had to leave his driver's license with her. He wasn't quite sure if he was mistreated, so he asked if I could go to the same counter and see the same woman and ask to see diamonds. Even though I unfortunately had no one to propose to, I obliged and a half hour later at 2:00 in the afternoon I had five diamonds on the counter at once with no request to turn in my driver's license. I felt angry for Reggie, but it still didn't dawn on me that I somehow was making out like a bandit for being treated like a normal human being. Reggie even had a nicer suit on than me. I doubt he had to give his license simply because he was six feet tall and I was barely pushing five-foot nine.

The phrase white privilege immediately focuses on the life of the so-called privileged person, and not on what is taking place to people who are disadvantaged in society. "Black detriment" more accurately reflects what has been taking place. The daily occurrences black folks experience that are unfair and unjust. When my friend Rick, a banker, was asked to step out of his vehicle for speeding in St. Louis and cops searched his car, removed his bucket seats, then left them on the side of the road for Rick to re-install, that was not about white privilege. It was about racism and unjust treatment.

This morning I went to Aviano to grab my coffee. "Hey, Jeffrey, good morning." I was greeted by Patrick with smiles and a recommendation on the new Ethiopian blend. "I love the shirt," one of the new baristas, Rebecca, told me as she laughed. It was Chanukah and my t-shirt read "Jews Do It For Eight Nights." Then off to my gym to work off the half almond croissant I just ate. A few fist pumps from a couple strangers when I walked in the door. "Jeffrey!" the owner smiled at me as I put my stuff in a locker. An hour later, I stopped at my cleaners down the street to drop off a few items and our grape juice stained Thanksgiving table cloth. "Good morning, Jeffrey. You have a few items you forgot to pick up." Finally, off to work, as I drove down 17th Avenue as a car let me in his lane. Fifteen minutes later I parked in the garage next to the sixty-story skyscraper where my law firm is located. Good mornings from Edward, the shoe shine guy, and Michael, who runs the security desk. I swiped my elevator access card and off to the fortieth floor to start my work day. Several more good morning exchanges with our receptionist Sonja, my assistant Kathleen, and a couple of lawyers walking down the hall. What a privileged morning, I thought. Ha! Not exactly. I didn't think twice about what had transpired that typical Wednesday morning. Life in the world of a white guy. How delightful.

Let's rethink our use of words so we can achieve a society where the majority recognizes the pain and experience of the minority, rather than focus on how bad people are for just living a normal life.

Justice, justice, shall you pursue – Babylonian Talmud

17

Trumped!

"You don't think Trump's a racist, do you?"

Regina and I were on our second date and the black couple next to us at Kazoku Sushi in Lakewood, Colorado was discussing the issue of Trump's racism rather loudly over a tray of yellowtail, eel, and salmon sushi rolls. I only noticed because eel creeps me out. I must have smirked at the couple's remarks when Regina came at me hard with her question. We had such a nice first date and I really had no reason to suspect Regina was a hardcore Trump supporter.

Our first date was at a quaint place just outside of downtown Denver. I remember it well. Regina stood up to hug me when I arrived five minutes late. She was an inch taller than me at almost five-foot ten, had alluring dark eyes, long eyelashes, and a stunning body. She gave me a peck on the cheek. "So nice to meet you," she said with an approving smile. "You're cute!" I was flattered. I guess my working out and eating right the past six months was paying off. We had met on the online dating app Bumble, so that was the first time either of us saw more than pictures. Regina and I talked and talked for almost two hours. About our families. College. Exercise. Our jobs. Things we like to do. It couldn't have gone better. She was gorgeous, nice, and smart. The perfect combo! We set a second date before we said our goodbyes. "I'd like to see you before you go out of town this Friday, Jeffrey." "How about this Thursday?" I asked. She checked her phone and the date was booked.

"Well, of course I think he's racist," I responded in a calm tone to her question about Trump.

This is when things went south. And I mean really south.

"Why the fucking hell would you think that?!" she asked me in an angry tone, the decibel rising with each word.

I'm not sure why some Trump supporters feel the need to respond with such vigor, volume and anger. While I try to avoid these types of discussions in general, I definitely had noticed a pattern of more aggressive reactions when anything related to Trump comes up. I usually just refer to him as forty-five anyway. I've never had so much disdain for a president, so I can't always muster the word "president" in connection with Trump.

I continued in my calm tone, despite wanting to turn up the volume to match hers.

"First, Trump hired Steve Bannon to be one of his top advisors after he was elected. Bannon is the chairman of the far right-wing, racist, and anti-Semitic publication *Breitbart News*. That was enough to raise my eyebrows."

It only took this one statement for the defend-Trump-at-all-costs response to follow.

"Trump probably didn't even know about his connection to that publication," she yelled at me with piercing eyes. "Anyway, he's doing a great job as president."

I remained relaxed, reminding her that I wasn't commenting about the job he was doing or not doing.

"Didn't know Bannon was head of a racist publication?" I retorted. "Even I knew in Denver, Colorado. And I'm nobody."

"He's an important man. I'm sure someone else was handling it for him. President Trump doesn't have time for all that," she continued with adamant defense.

"C'mon, it was in every newspaper in America," I shrugged. "Plus, who hired the person allegedly handling it for him? Trump? Or another staffer?"

Realizing her initial line of defense might have sounded a bit off, she switched gears.

"Anyway, how do you know that publication is racist? You can't believe everything you read on the internet. Everyone knows that!"

I almost couldn't contain myself but I proceeded even more calmly than I started despite her loud defenses. Other patrons in the restaurant had begun to stare.

"Um… I was just going by what his alt-right publication says in opposing multiculturalism and immigration and their claim about Jewish conspiracies for white genocide. You can read the articles yourself. It's their own words. I'm not making this shit up."

"Well, I try to avoid reading stuff on the internet," she exclaimed as if she "got" me, and somehow there was another mysterious source for all this information I was missing out on.

Just to make sure she knew it wasn't just one thing, I couldn't hold back further.

"Trump's also said that some people marching along Nazis in Charlottesville were very fine people. He called African countries shit holes. One of his speech writers is a regular attendee at alt-right conferences. The American Nazi Party and David Duke are among his supporters…"

She couldn't take it anymore, even though I wasn't finished with my long list.

"It's not his fault bad people support him. How's he supposed to control that?" she interrupted.

I couldn't believe I had to explain more to this highly intelligent, educated woman.

"All he had to do was forcefully disavow these hate groups. He's never done so in any meaningful way. Instead, choosing people from their ranks. He knows they voted for him. He knows they're part of his base. He'll gladly take their votes even if it means giving racists a voice."

"I think you should get the check," she snapoed at me as she threw her napkin on the table in disgust. "Or maybe we should just agree to disagree."

"What is it exactly we are agreeing to disagree on?" I asked sarcastically, but still in my annoying-calm tone.

I motioned for the waiter and handed her my credit card before asking for the check. She demanded to split the bill, but it's not my style so I paid for dinner anyway and we headed to our respective cars. The waiter gave me an "I feel for you" look as she had heard almost the entire exchange. I imagine half the restaurant did.

"Well, I know it didn't work out, but I wish you the best," I told her and then headed to my car without so much as a handshake goodbye.

A text message popped up on my phone minutes later.

"You obviously are someone who cannot handle someone with different views."

I couldn't help but laugh since my friend circle always includes people across the political spectrum.

I should have let it go, but I texted back.

"So the thing is, racism isn't a different view. I'm great friends with people with different opinions on economics, the environment, foreign policy, taxes, etc. I don't do well with racism. It's a disease, not a viewpoint. Best of luck to you."

I suppose I owe forty-five a little thanks. Three days later, a woman I had adored so much reached out for the first time in a month and asked if I wanted to try and make things work, and Regina wasn't in the way. Maybe Trump serves a good purpose after all.

(*Nah.*)

About the Author

Jeffrey is an author, lawyer and community activist residing in Denver, Colorado.

He earned his undergraduate degree from The Ohio State University in 1992, where he was a member of the prestigious senior honor society, Sphinx. He also was recognized by then President of Ohio State, Gordon Gee, for his leadership contributions. In 1991, he was selected as one of five members of Ohio State's Homecoming Court. Jeffrey frequently refers to himself as half Jewish, half Buckeye. Jeffrey earned his J.D. from the University of Toledo in 1995, where he graduated cum laude and attended on a full academic scholarship. While in law school, he received multiple academic awards, was on the law review, served as president of one of the law student associations, and was editor of the law student newspaper.

Jeffrey has been writing and publishing works since college. Over the past 25 years, he has authored over 100 articles on issues such as Israel, race, politics, law and religion. His works have been published in both major and regional publications over the years, including several pieces in the *St. Louis Post Dispatch*, *The Utah Star Tribune*, the *Connecticut Jewish Ledger*, *The St. Louis Jewish Light*, *The Ohio Jewish Chronicle*, *Visions* and others. Professionally, Jeffrey has authored dozens of articles and a book on intellectual property legal issues over the past 20 years. He also is a national speaker, having engaged local and national audiences on intellectual property issues, as well as issues facing startup companies. Jeffrey is a guest-lecturer at Washington University, UCLA and The University of Colorado-Denver. He also has done amateur standup comedy since he was 18.

In 2016, Jeffrey pivoted and focused his writing on entertainment writing, primarily in the genre he likes to call "Traumedy." Taking real-life, sometimes difficult, situations and throwing in a dose of crass humor. His writing is intended to engage, challenge, inspire, sometimes even offend and make people think and laugh. His short story essay writings have earned him multiple writing awards in international competitions over the past several years. In 2018, he was nominated for the a prestigious American literary award called the Pushcart Prize for his story "Staycation," which is chapter one of an upcoming book, *Sheldon & Irene, A Traumedy.*

In his legal career, Jeffrey is a partner at the national law firm of Lewis Brisbois where he is an intellectual property trial lawyer. In that role, he has been honored as a *Super Lawyer* for several years (a recognition only given to 5% of the nation's lawyers) and in 2016 he was named by *The National Law Journal* as one of the top trailblazing lawyers in his field. He also has been advising startup and emerging companies for the past 20 years. *Small Business Monthly* named Jeffrey one of the Top Ten Lawyers for Entrepreneurs. Today he is general counsel to over 40 such companies nationwide. In addition to his legal practice, Jeffrey has been an adjunct professor teaching intellectual property litigation, he is involved in a number of civic organizations and he volunteers countless hours to his community by volunteering at a Camp Mak-A-Dream, a camp for kids with cancer in Montana, tutoring and reading to kids in the public schools in St. Louis and Denver, and helping feed the homeless. He also has been involved with civil rights issues for the better part of his professional career, having served on the boards of the ADL and Urban League in St. Louis. He currently sits on the boards of the Urban Leadership Foundation of Colorado, Denver Delta, Inc. and Youth Roots. He also has helped lead groups of elected officials to Israel to teach them about the country and the issues facing the Middle East.

In his "free time," Jeffrey is an avid reader, exerciser, chef, storyteller, hiker, traveler, philosopher, fashionista and coffee connoisseur.

Above all, Jeffrey is a proud and active father to three kind, compassionate, smart, fun, engaging and loving children.